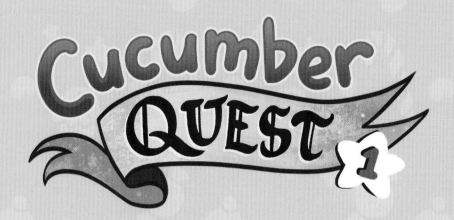

# The Doughnut Kingdom

## Gigi D.G.

First Second
New York

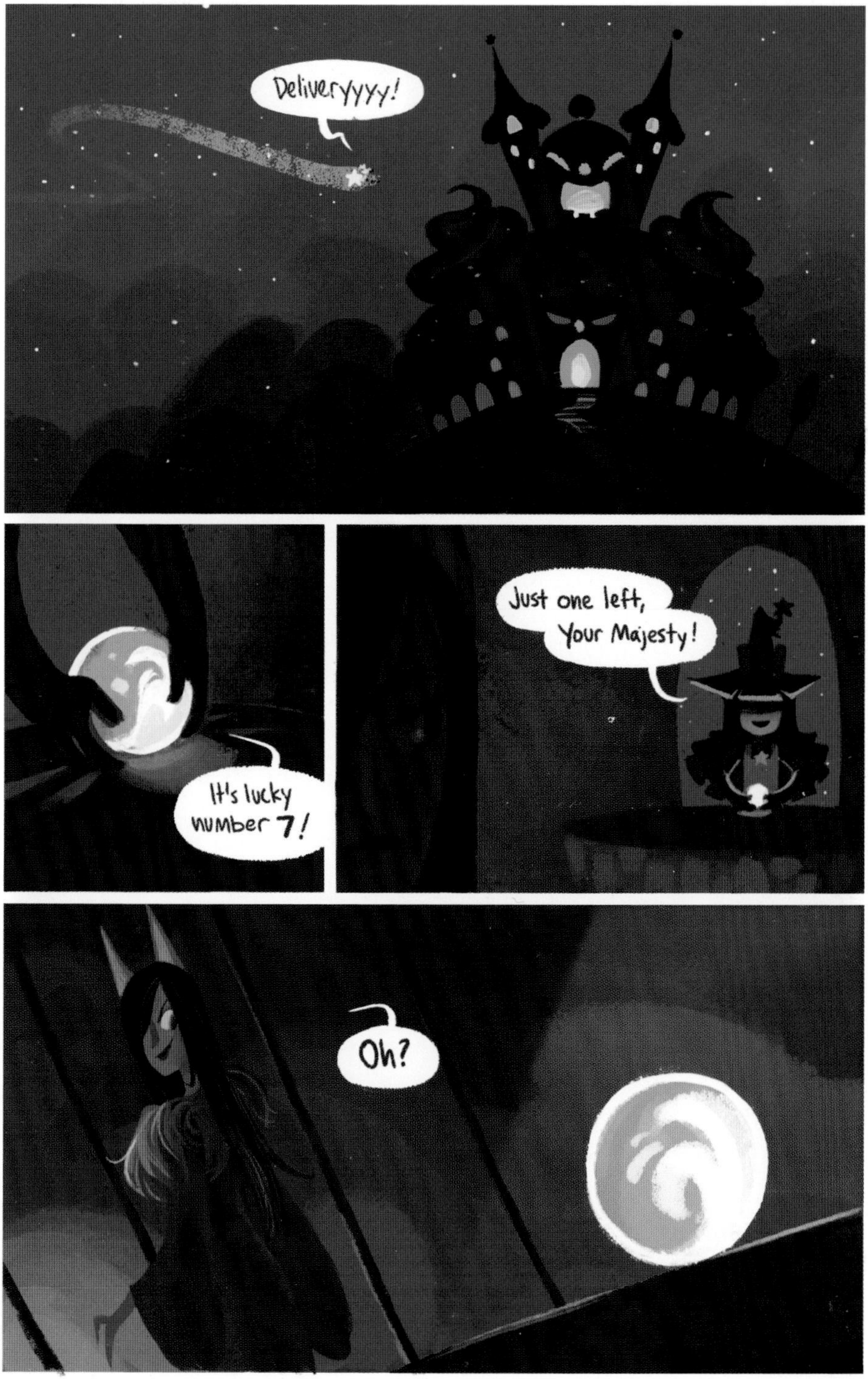
Deliveryyyy!
It's lucky number 7!
Just one left, Your Majesty!
Oh?

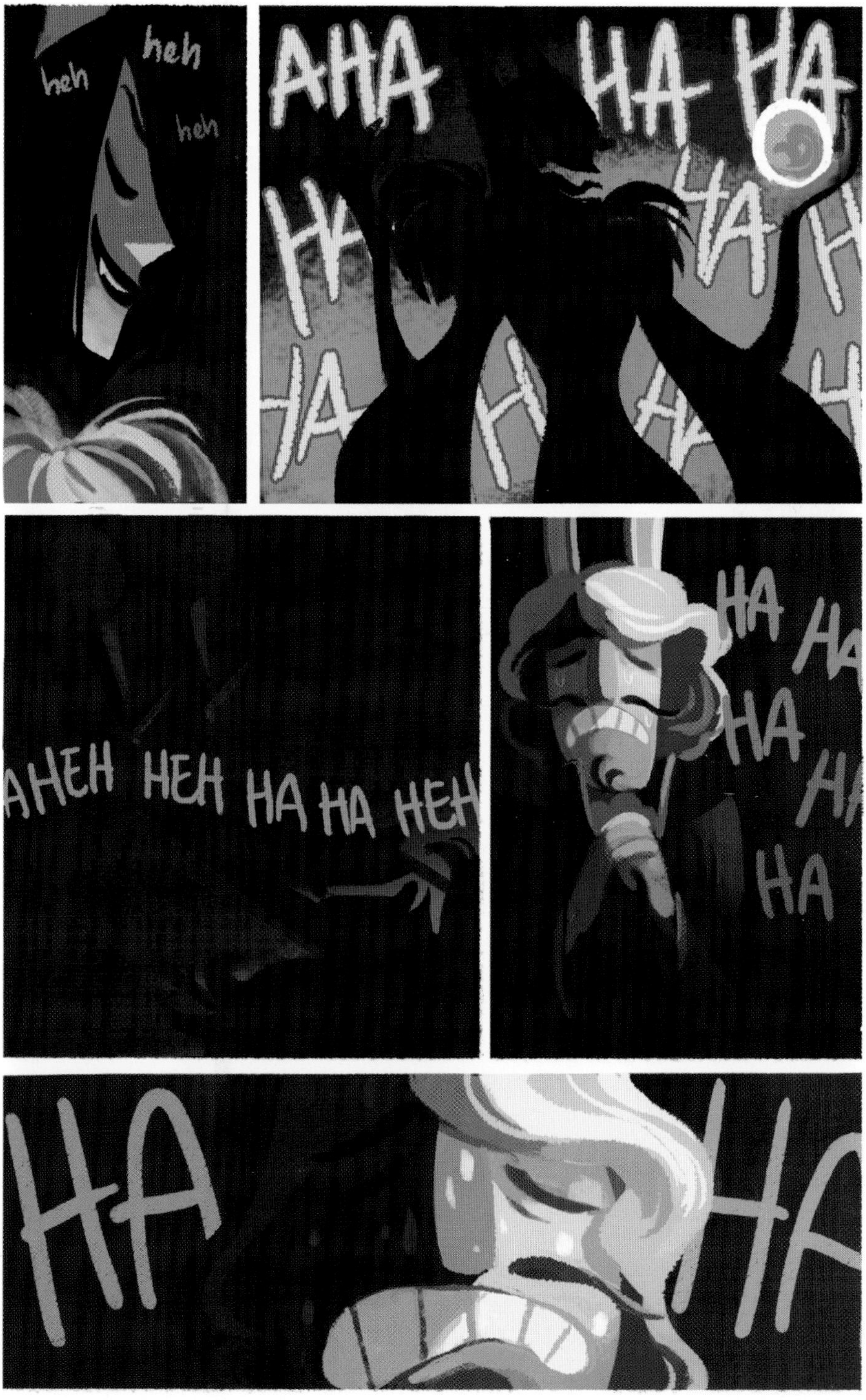
heh
heh
heh
AHA
HA HA
HA
HA
AHEH HEH HA HA HEH
HA
HA
HA
HA
HA
HA
HA

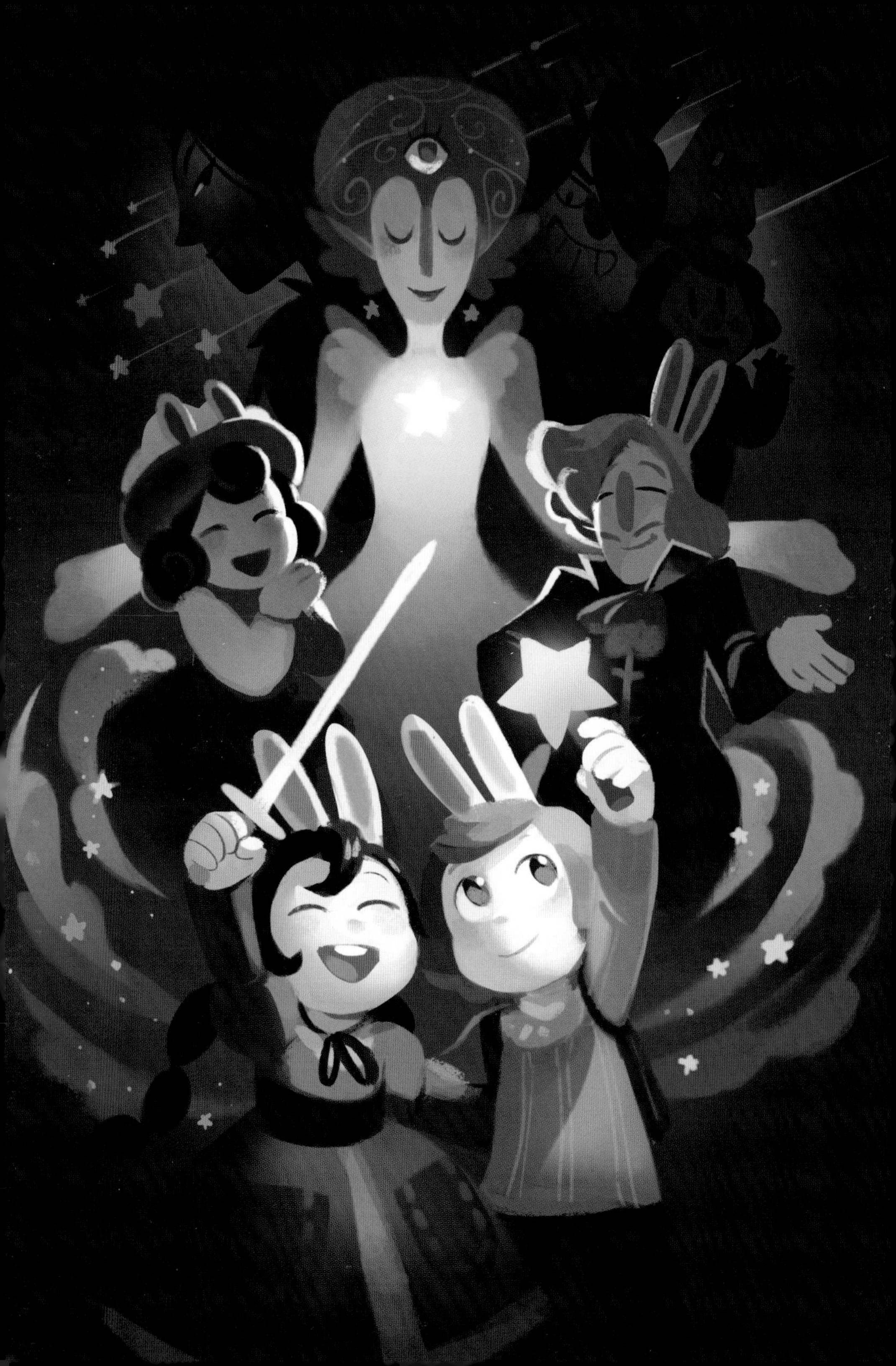

# PROLOGUE

Thanks, Mom and Dad!

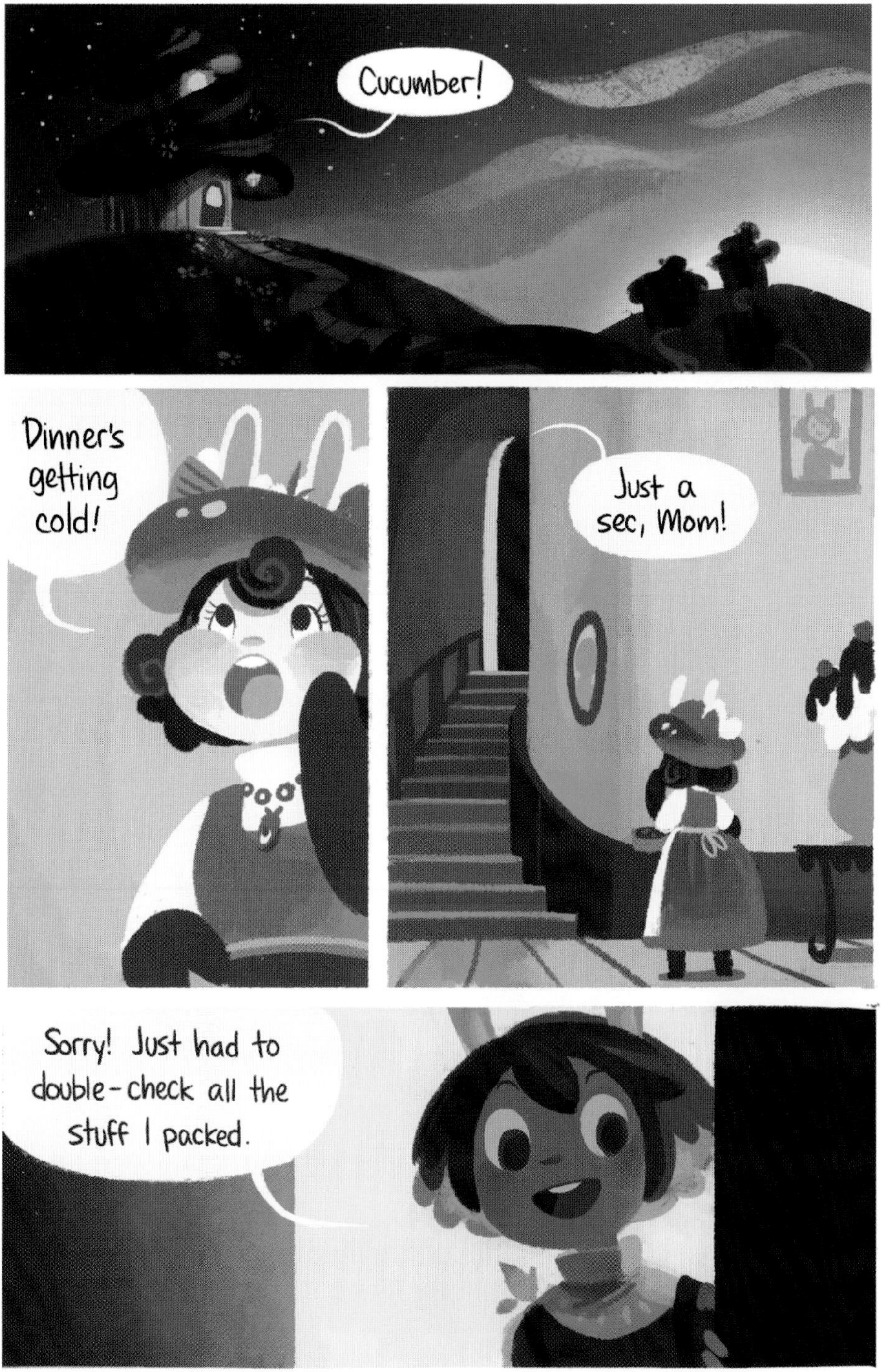
Cucumber!
Dinner's getting cold!
Just a sec, Mom!
Sorry! Just had to double-check all the stuff I packed.

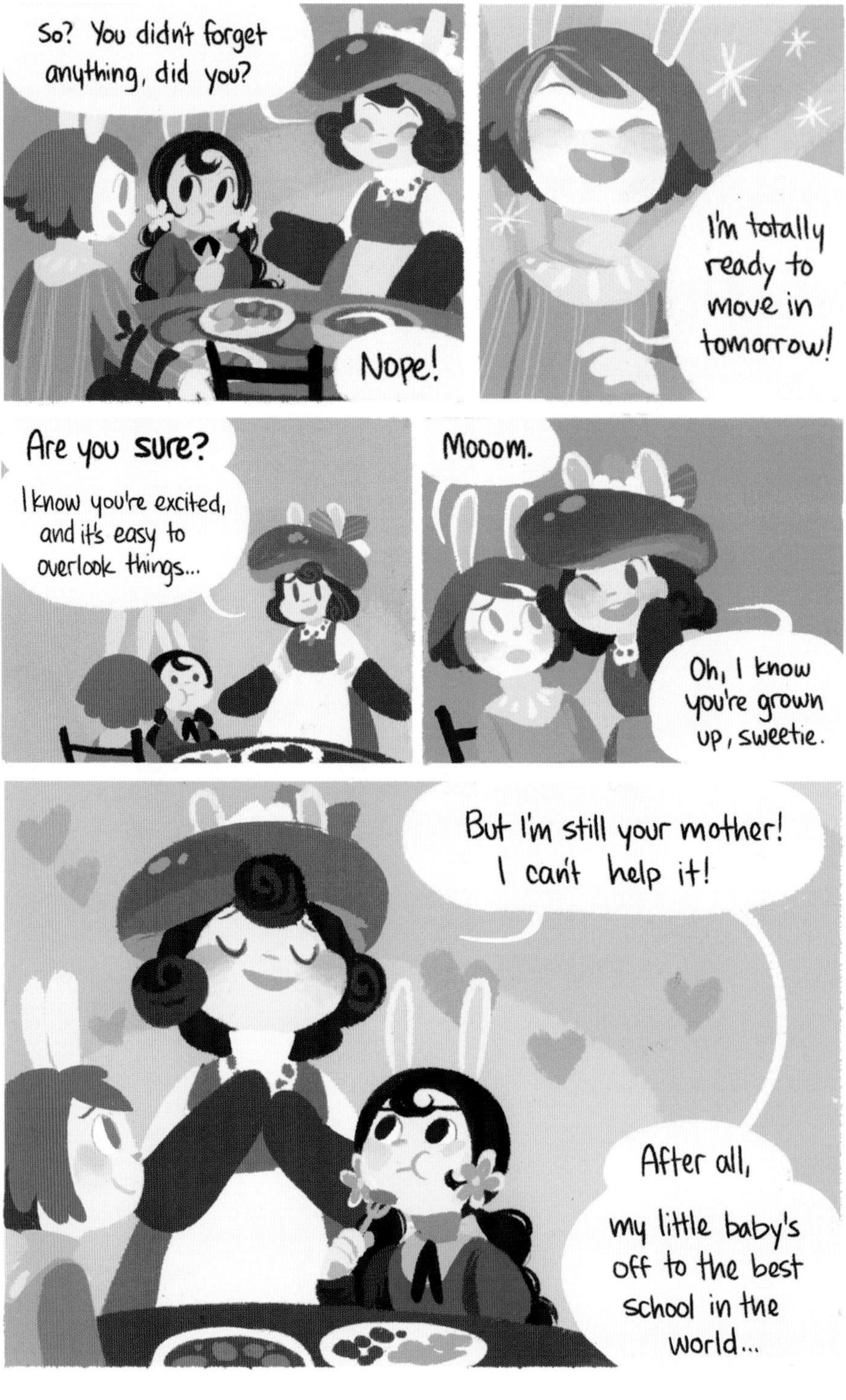
So? You didn't forget anything, did you?
Nope!
I'm totally ready to move in tomorrow!
Are you sure?
I know you're excited, and it's easy to overlook things...
Mooom.
Oh, I know you're grown up, sweetie.
But I'm still your mother! I can't help it!
After all,
my little baby's off to the best school in the world...

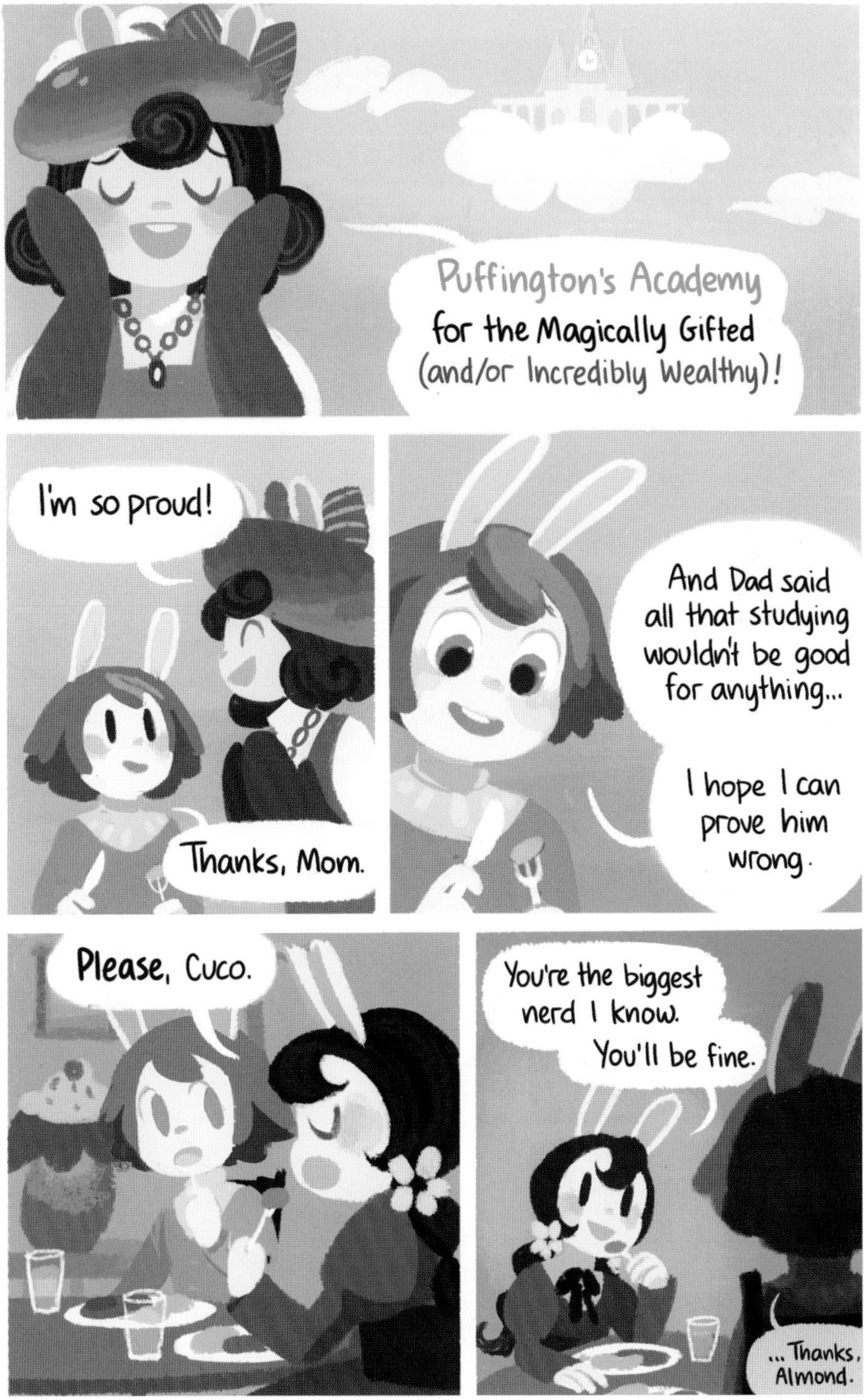
Puffington's Academy for the Magically Gifted (and/or Incredibly Wealthy)!
I'm so proud!
Thanks, Mom.
And Dad said all that studying wouldn't be good for anything...
I hope I can prove him wrong.
Please, Cuco.
You're the biggest nerd I know.
You'll be fine.
...Thanks, Almond.

KNOCK
KNOCK

Oh! Now who could it be this late?

It's always when you sit down to eat dinner...

Evening, ma'am! Got a letter for you.

My!

Didn't we already get today's mail?

This one's a special delivery!

Royal Mail

Well, take care!

Oh—um, thank you!

10

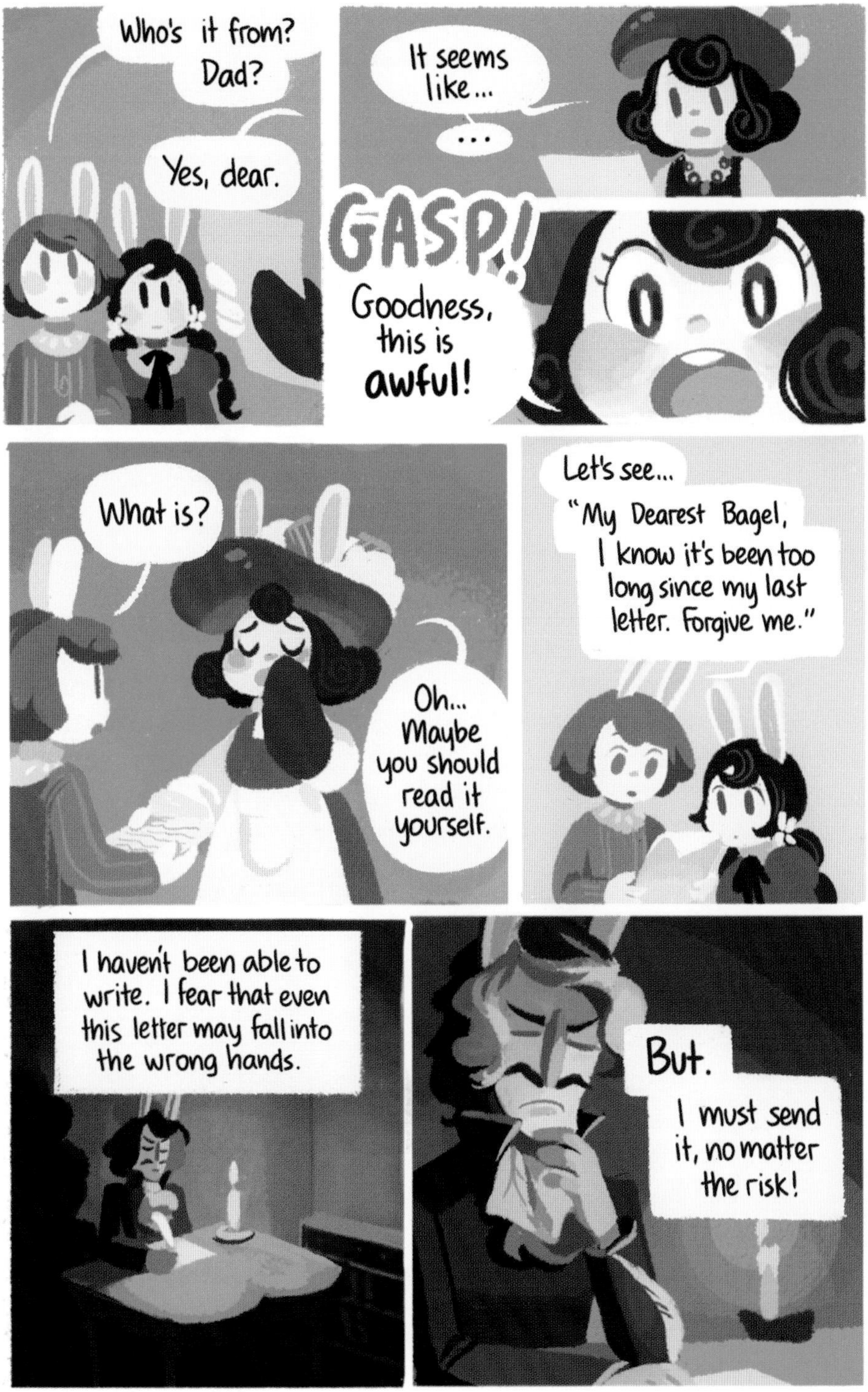

Who's it from? Dad?
Yes, dear.
It seems like...
...
GASP!
Goodness, this is **awful!**
What is?
Oh... Maybe you should read it yourself.
Let's see...
"My Dearest Bagel, I know it's been too long since my last letter. Forgive me."
I haven't been able to write. I fear that even this letter may fall into the wrong hands.
But.
I must send it, no matter the risk!

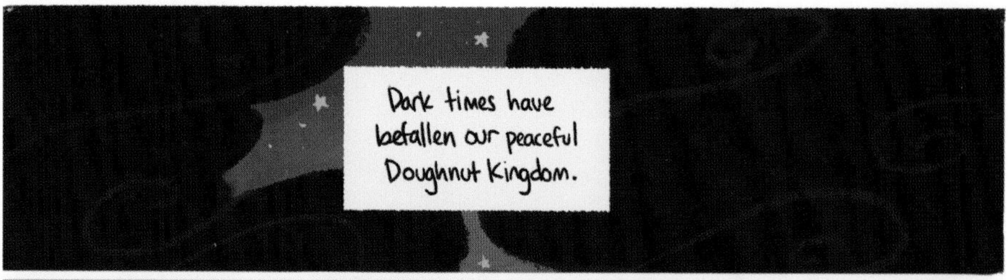
Dark times have befallen our peaceful Doughnut Kingdom.

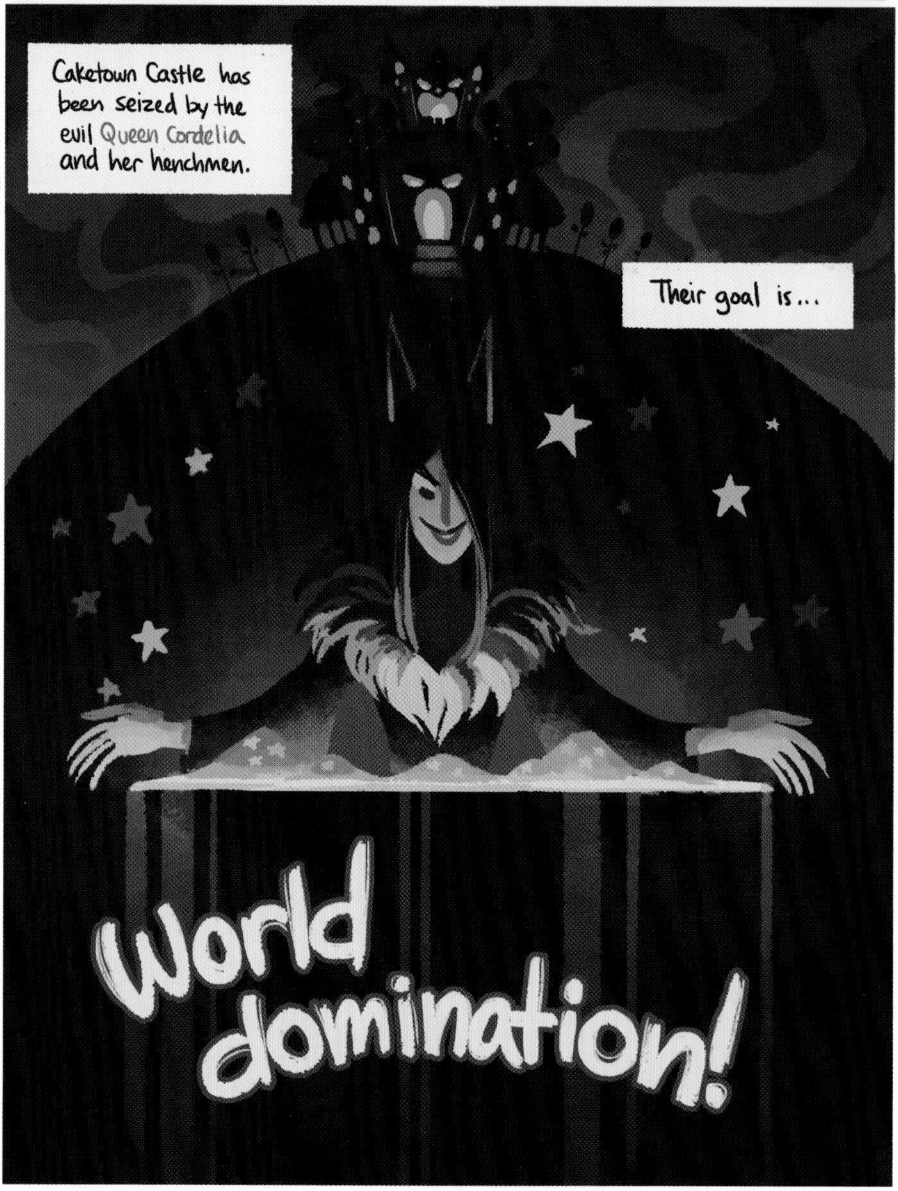
Caketown Castle has been seized by the evil Queen Cordelia and her henchmen.
Their goal is...
World domination!

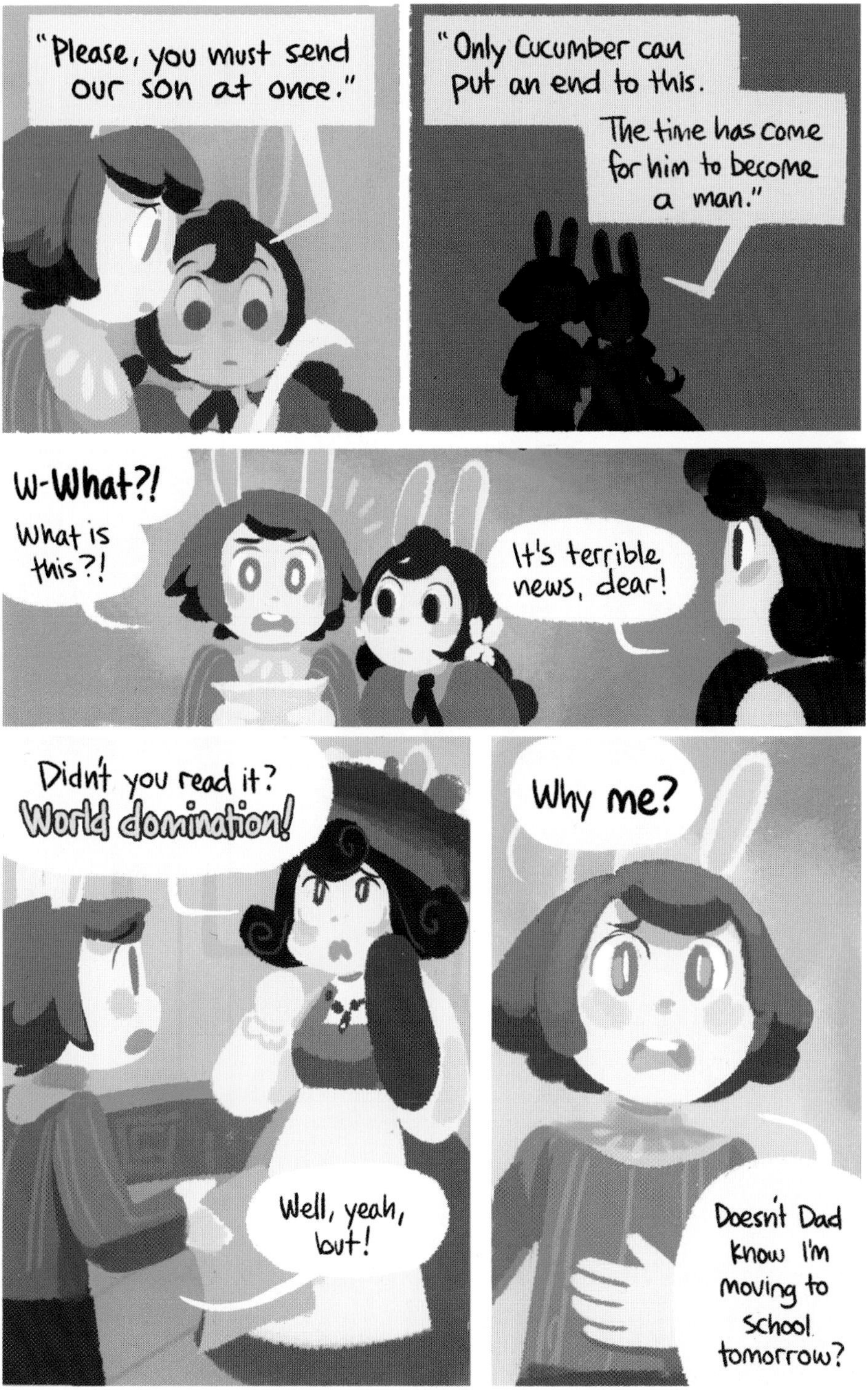
"Please, you must send our son at once."
"Only Cucumber can put an end to this.
The time has come for him to become a man."
W-What?!
What is this?!
It's terrible news, dear!
Didn't you read it? World domination!
Well, yeah, but!
Why me?
Doesn't Dad know I'm moving to school tomorrow?

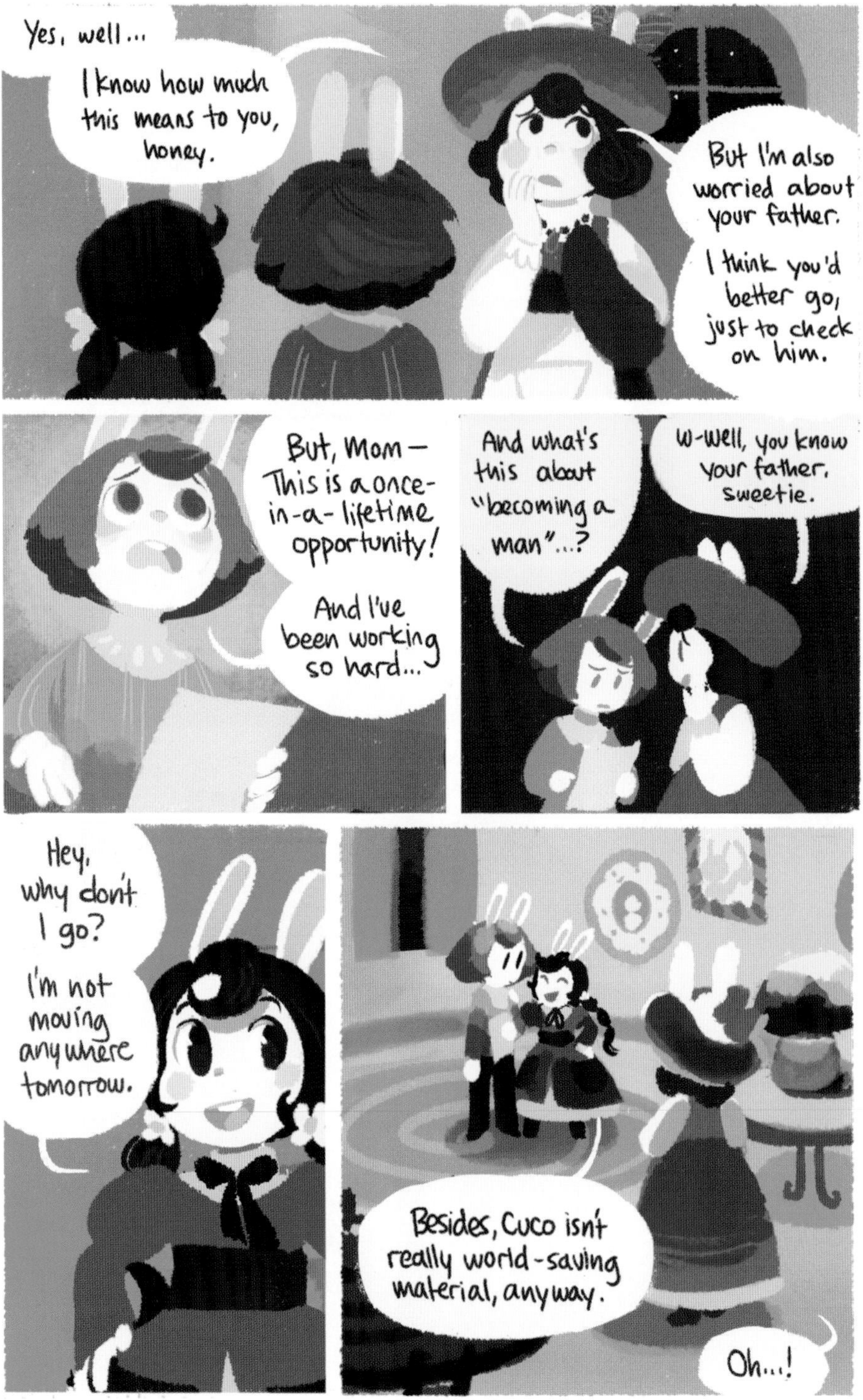
Yes, well...
I know how much this means to you, honey.
But I'm also worried about your father.
I think you'd better go, just to check on him.
But, Mom— This is a once-in-a-lifetime opportunity!
And I've been working so hard...
And what's this about "becoming a man"...?
W-Well, you know your father, sweetie.
Hey, why don't I go?
I'm not moving anywhere tomorrow.
Besides, Cuco isn't really world-saving material, anyway.
Oh...!

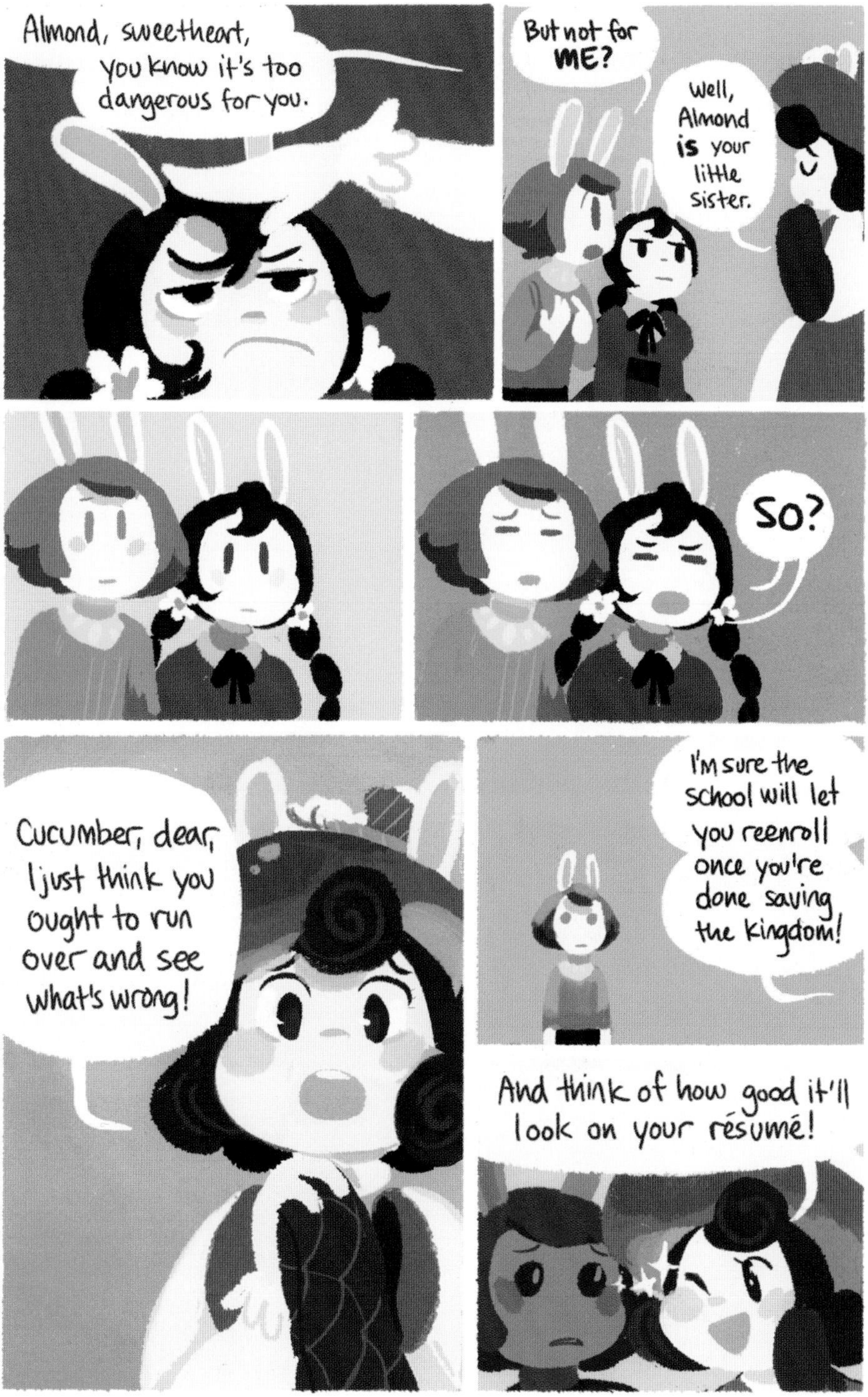
Almond, sweetheart, you know it's too dangerous for you.
But not for **ME?**
Well, Almond **is** your little sister.
SO?
Cucumber, dear, I just think you ought to run over and see what's wrong!
I'm sure the school will let you reenroll once you're done saving the kingdom!
And think of how good it'll look on your résumé!

Good thing you already packed your bag!

SHOVE

Oh, you look like a hero already.

But I didn't even finish—

Go get 'em, sweetie!

And be sure to write!

BUT—!

SLAM!

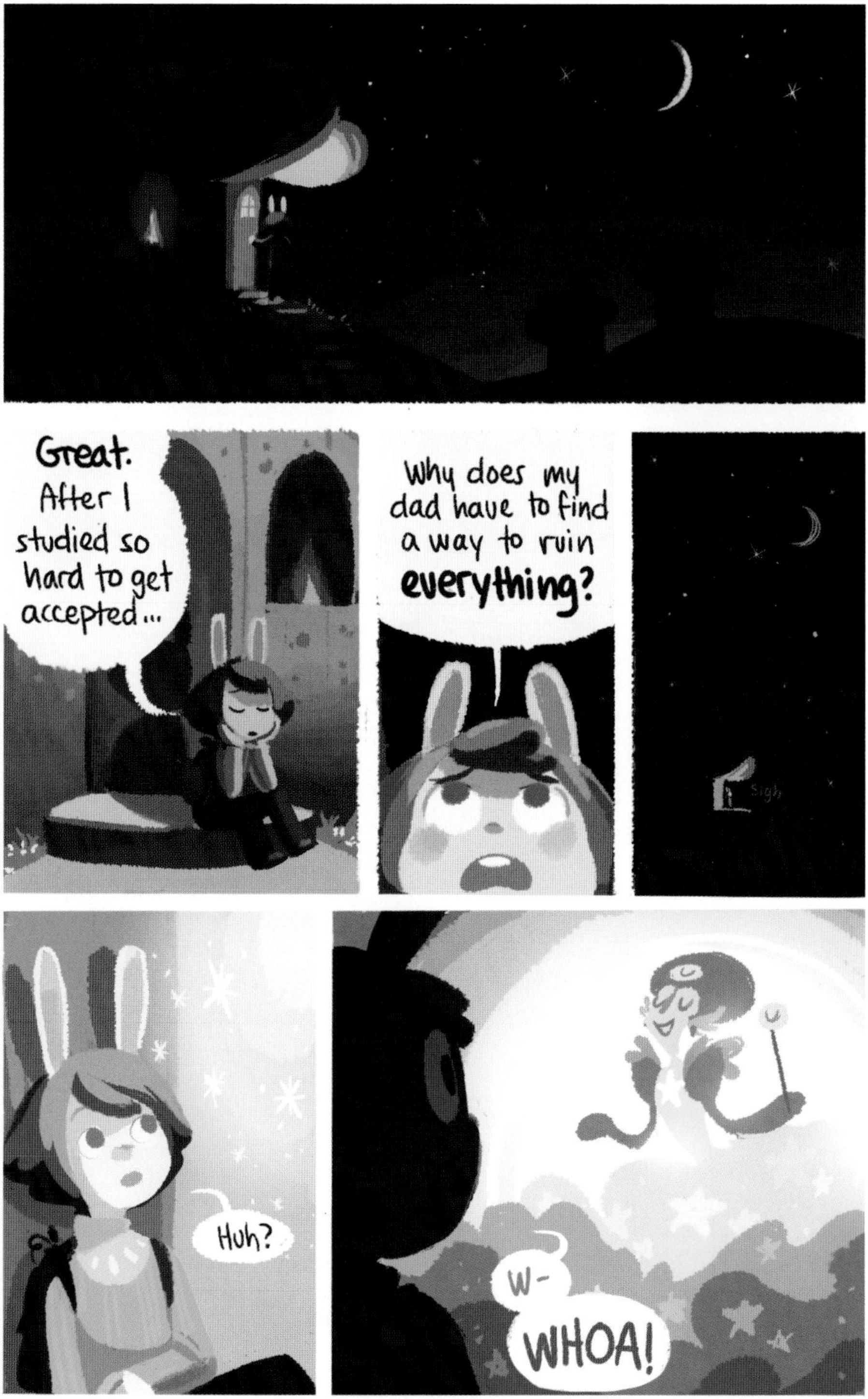
Great. After I studied so hard to get accepted...
Why does my dad have to find a way to ruin **everything?**
Sigh
Huh?
W-
WHOA!

At last I've found you...

Legendary Hero!

Huh? No, I—

Now, now! No need to be modest!

You **are** Cucumber, son of Lord Cabbage, are you not?

W-Well, yes, but—

Excellent!

I am the Dream Oracle, protector of this world!

I have **important information** regarding your **heroic quest.**

That's...great and everything, but...

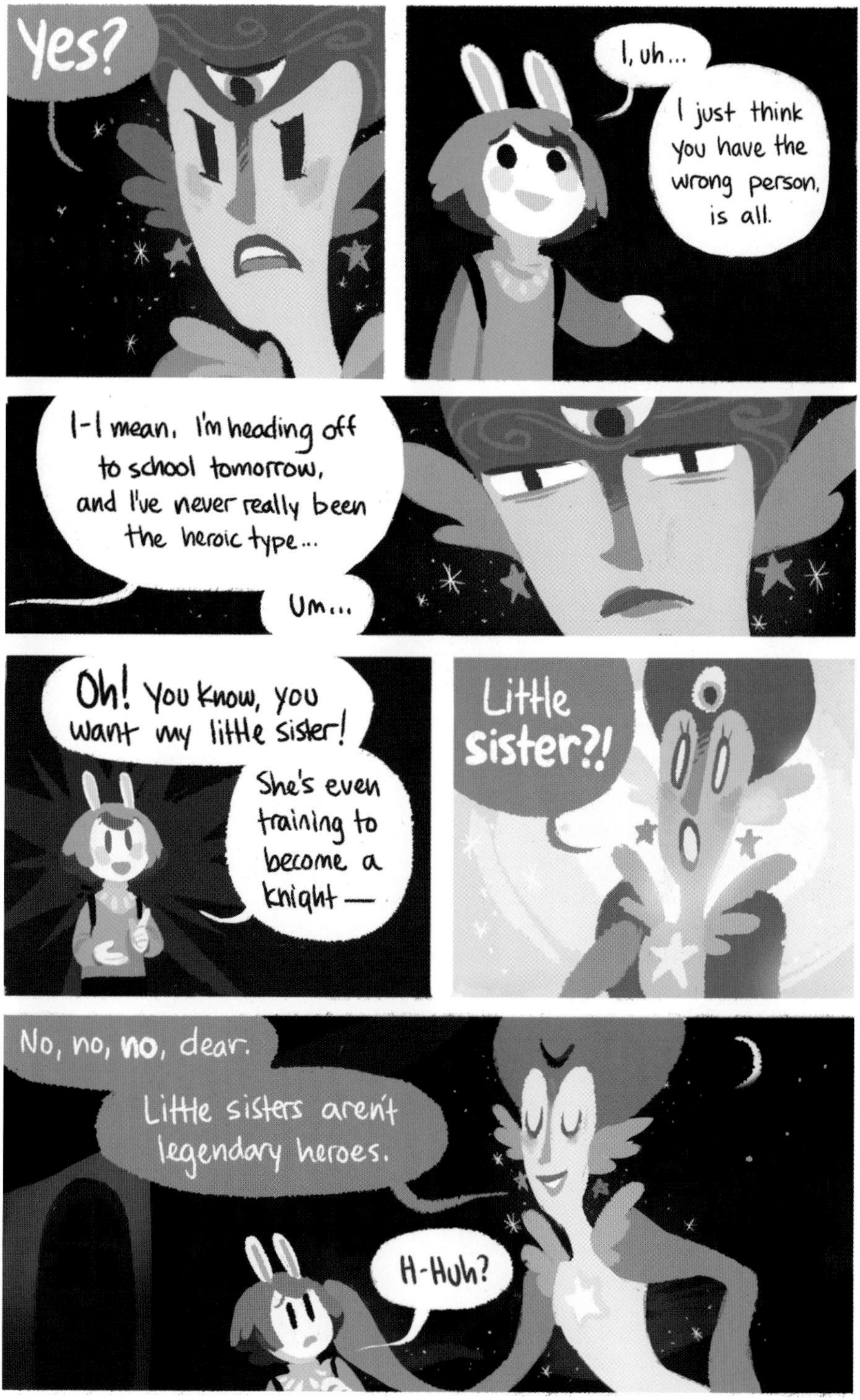
Yes?
I, uh...
I just think you have the wrong person, is all.
I-I mean. I'm heading off to school tomorrow, and I've never really been the heroic type...
Um...
Oh! You know, you want my little sister!
She's even training to become a knight—
Little sister?!
No, no, no, dear.
Little sisters aren't legendary heroes.
H-Huh?

20

And what I'm seeing right now...

... is that **YOU**, the hero, must restore peace to our world!

squish

Um.

Wait! Didn't you just say **YOU** were a "protector of this world"?

Can't you just defeat the ancient evil yourself?

W-What's that, dear?!

I think I'm losing reception!

21

Caketown

Well...

Here goes nothing, I guess...

23

Hold it.

Where do you think **YOU'RE** going, kid?

You can't just, like, barge into a castle, y'know?

Yeah!

Oh! I-I'm sorry!

Um, actually, I'm here to see my dad...

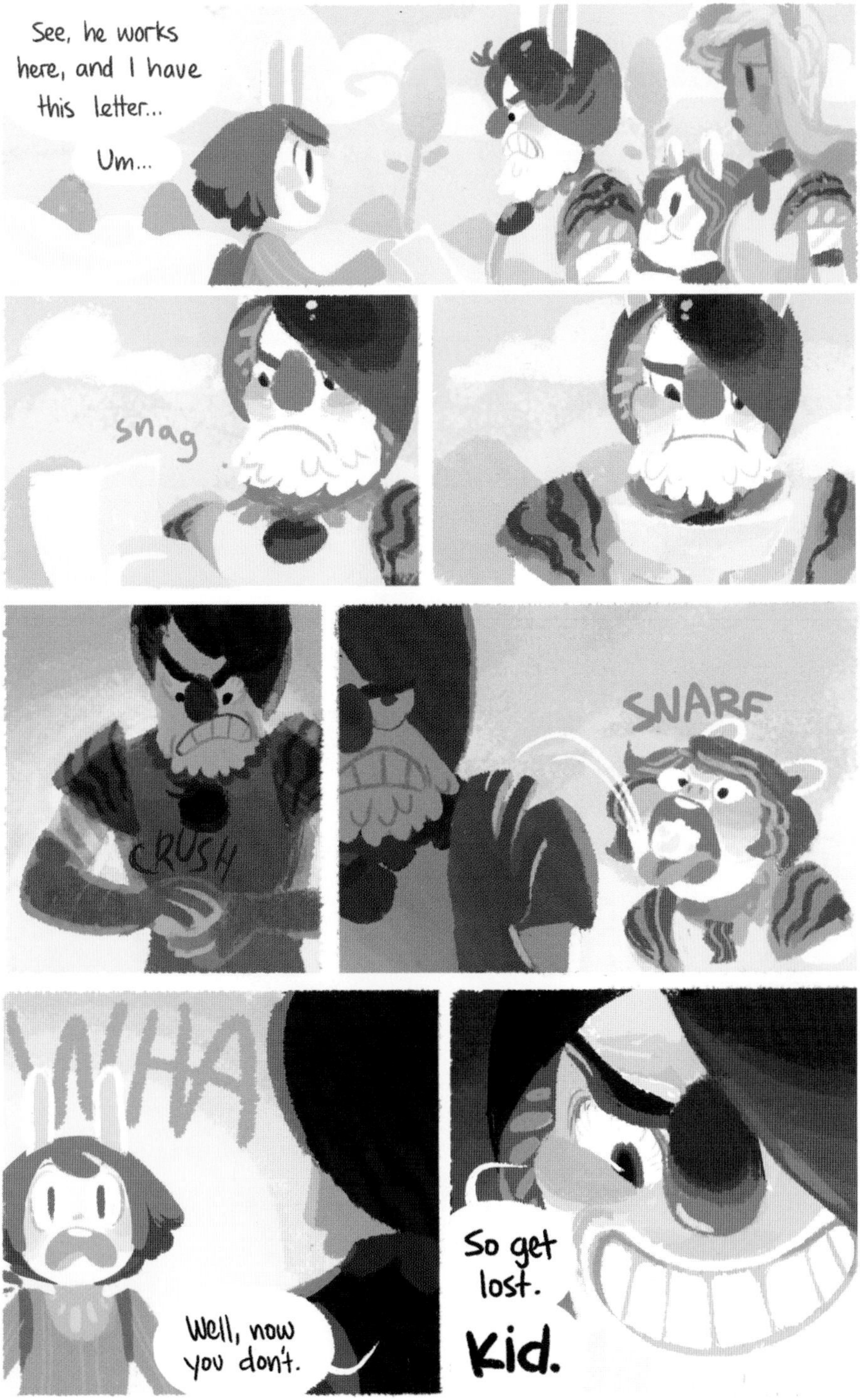
See, he works here, and I have this letter...
Um...
snag
CRUSH
SNARF
WHA
Well, now you don't.
So get lost.
Kid.

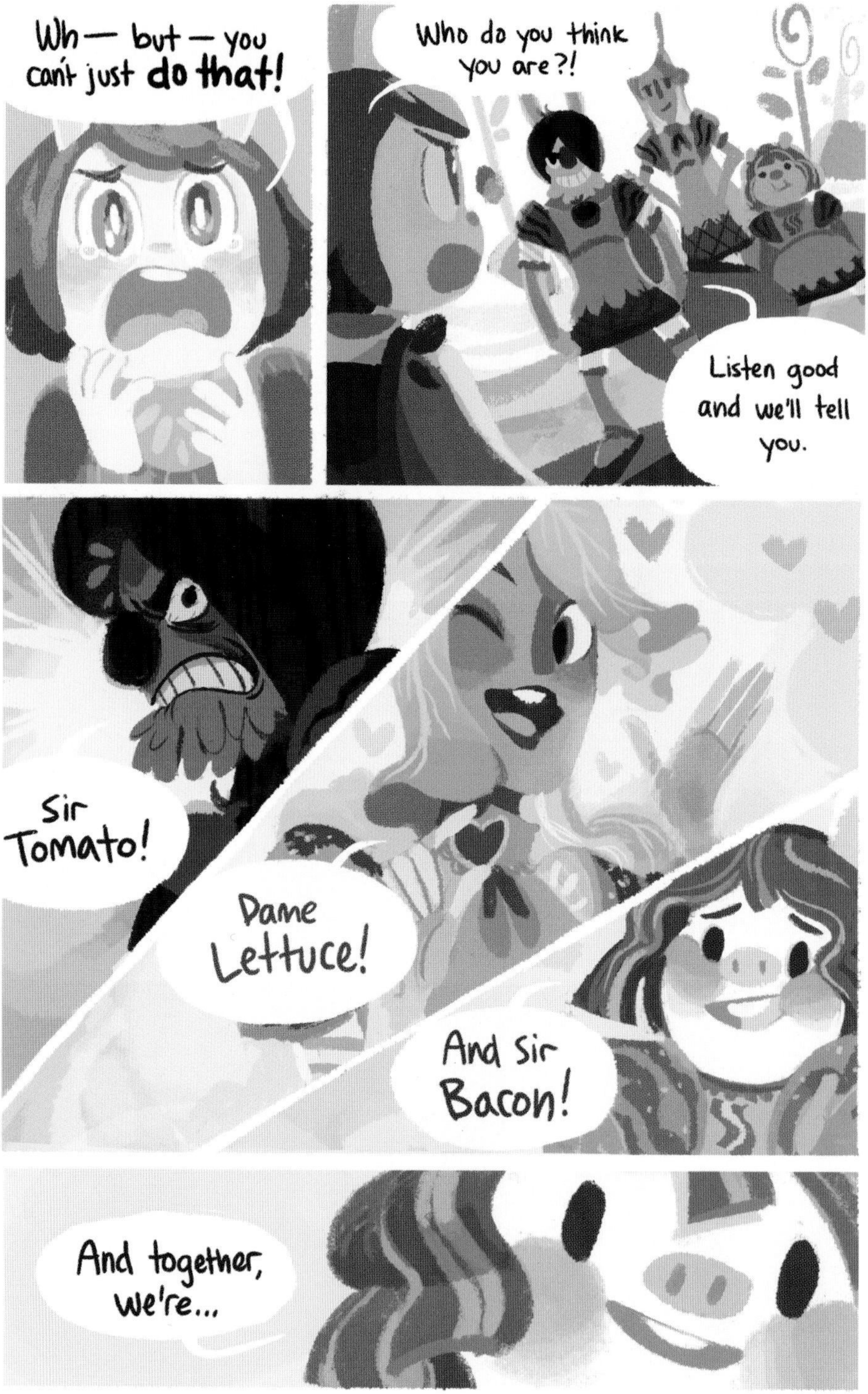
Wh— but— you can't just **do that!**
Who do you think you are?!
Listen good and we'll tell you.
Sir Tomato!
Dame Lettuce!
And Sir Bacon!
And together, we're...

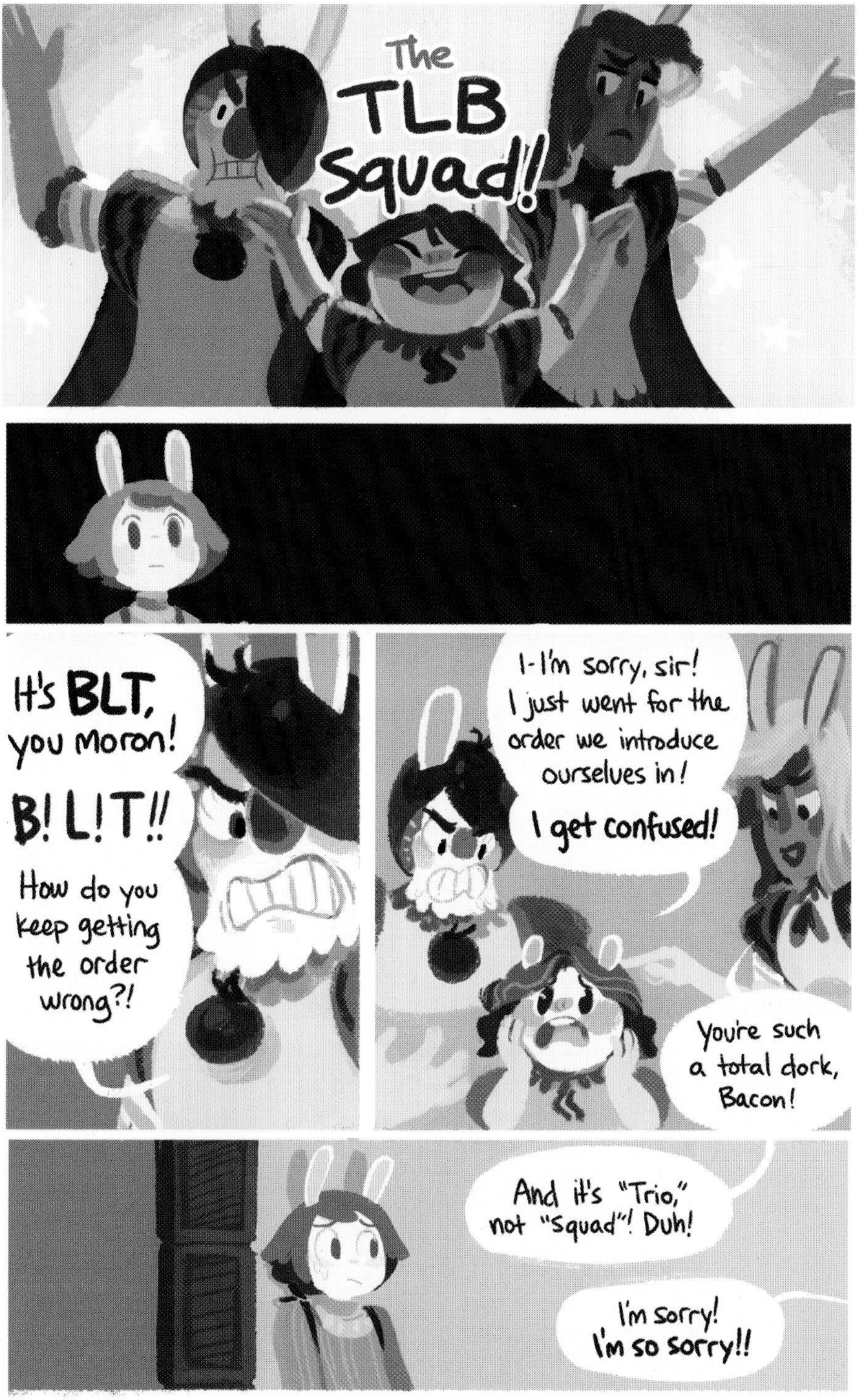
The TLB Squad!
It's BLT, you moron! B! L! T!! How do you keep getting the order wrong?!
I-I'm sorry, sir! I just went for the order we introduce ourselves in!
I get confused!
You're such a total dork, Bacon!
And it's "Trio," not "Squad"! Duh!
I'm sorry! I'm so sorry!!

Wow, what a bunch of freaks!

Maybe things are worse than I...

...huh?

Cucumber?

The most important day of your life has finally arrived...

The day you **become a man.**

Shut up and listen here, Cucumber, because this is serious.

Y-Yeah, you wrote that in the letter.

What does it even mean?

Well, Mister Read-the-Letter, you oughta know!

The world's in peril!

Peril?!

tweet
tweet

...Are you sure? It looks okay to me.

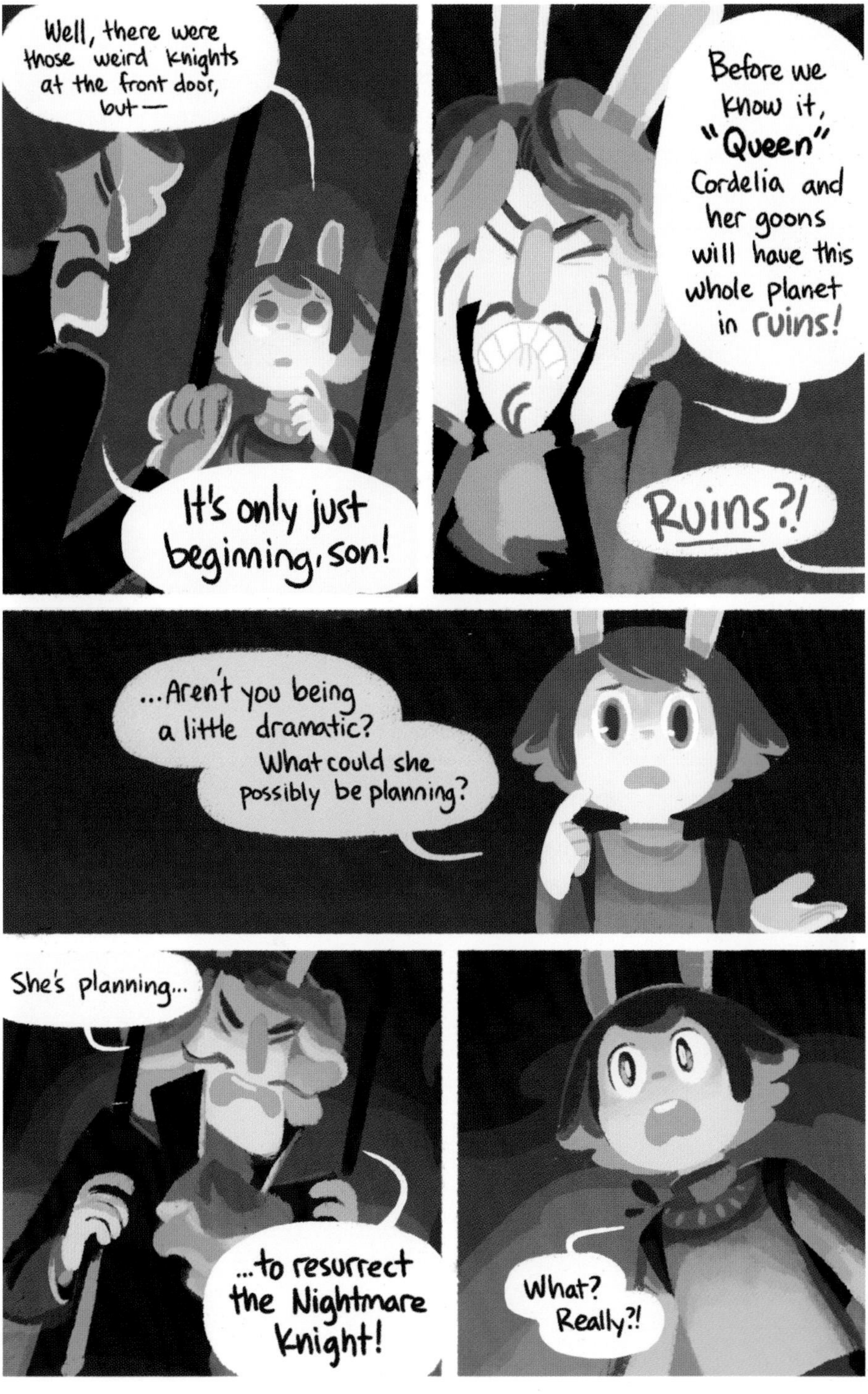
Well, there were those weird knights at the front door, but—
It's only just beginning, son!
Before we know it, "Queen" Cordelia and her goons will have this whole planet in ruins!
Ruins?!
...Aren't you being a little dramatic?
What could she possibly be planning?
She's planning...
...to resurrect the Nightmare Knight!
What? Really?!

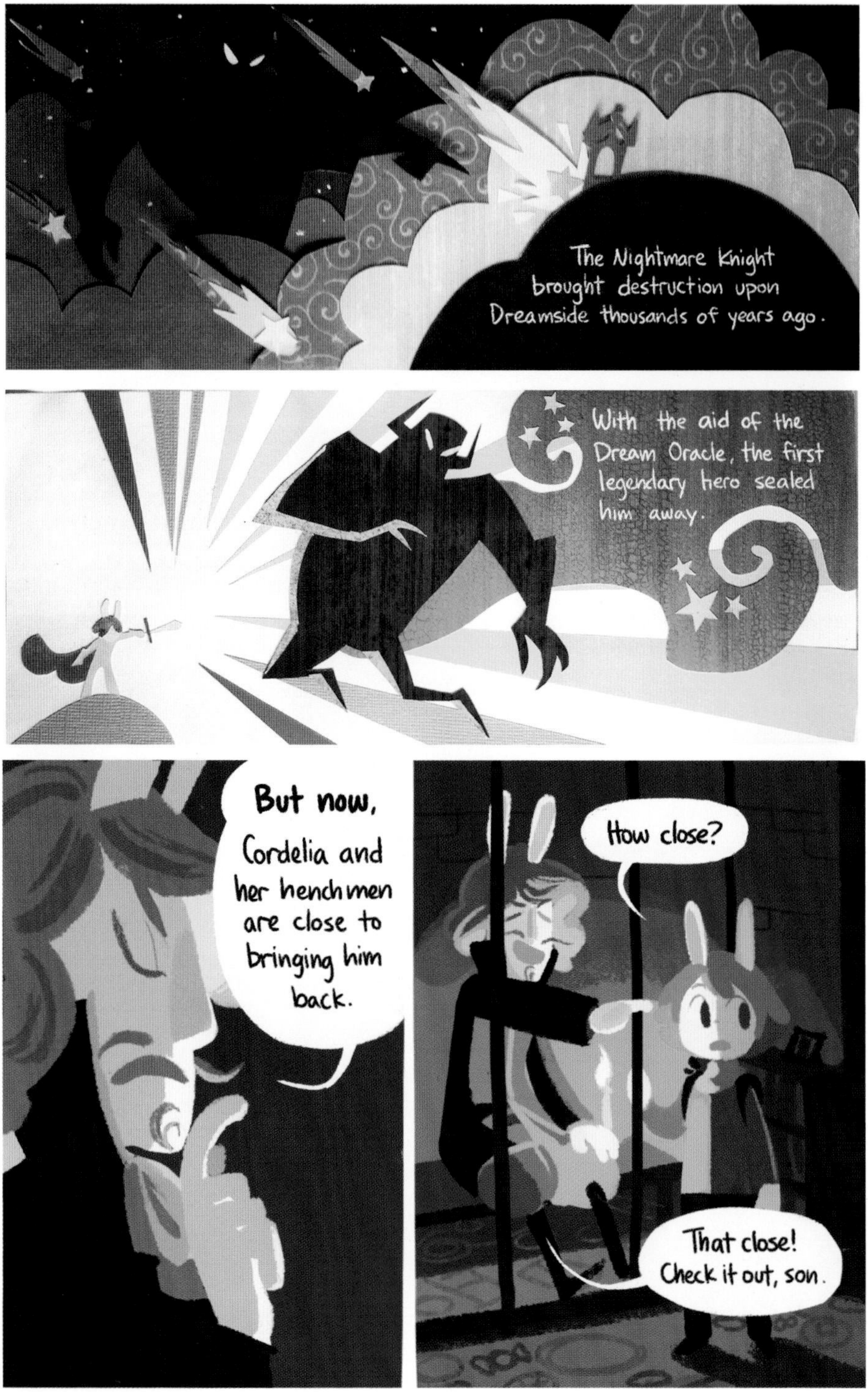

The Nightmare Knight brought destruction upon Dreamside thousands of years ago.
With the aid of the Dream Oracle, the first legendary hero sealed him away.
But now, Cordelia and her henchmen are close to bringing him back.
How close?
That close! Check it out, son.

Wait— **Sword?**

Dad, you know I've never held a sword in my life.

And how old are you, like, nine?* It's about time you learned how!

* nope

But Almond takes lessons!

Why don't I just run back home and tell her to—

**No!**
What? No!

Your little **sister,** Cucumber? Really?

When's the last time you ever heard of a little sister becoming a legendary hero?

Why does everybody keep—

**Absolutely not, son.**

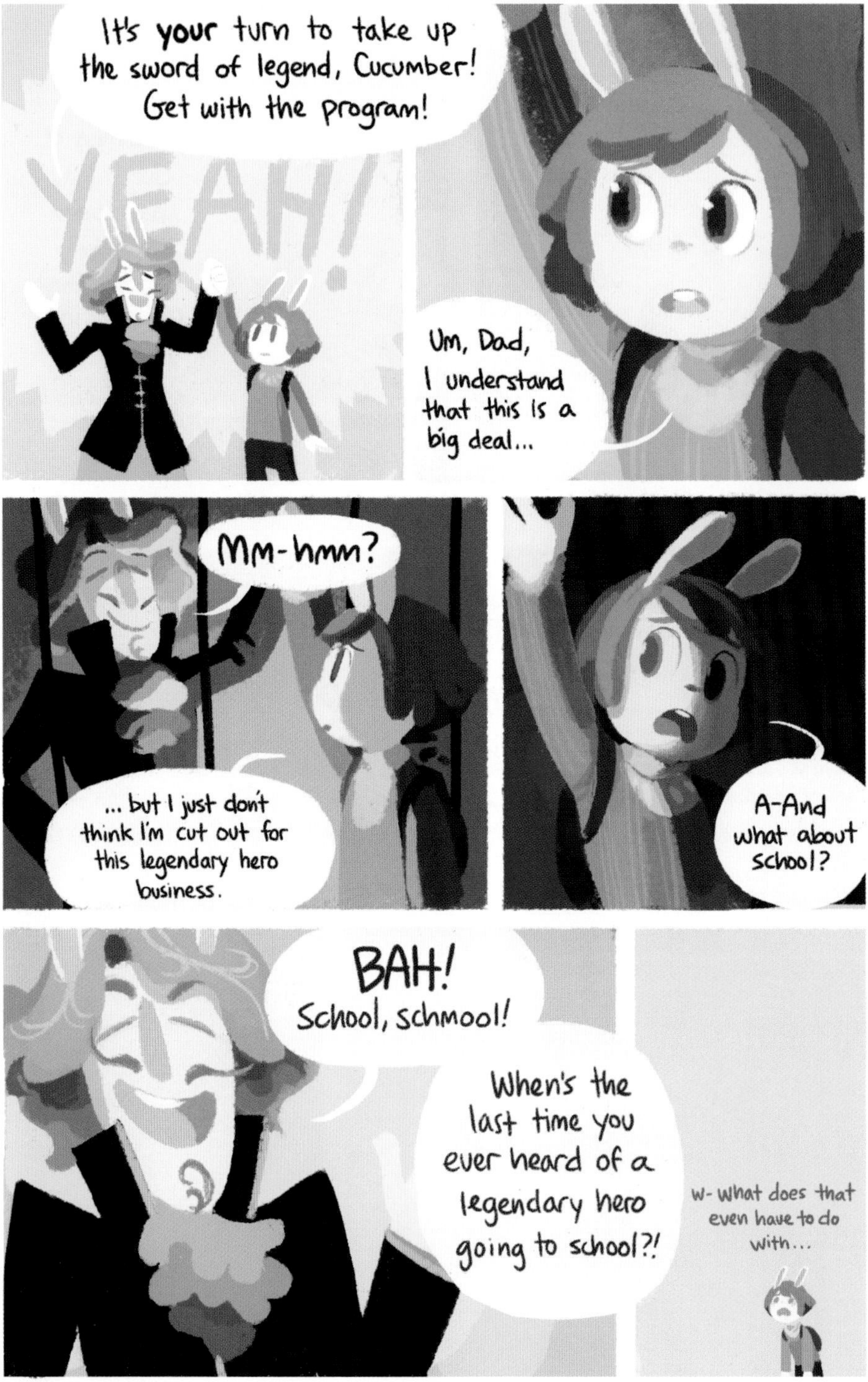
It's **your** turn to take up the sword of legend, Cucumber! Get with the program!
YEAH!
Um, Dad, I understand that this is a big deal...
Mm-hmm?
... but I just don't think I'm cut out for this legendary hero business.
A-And what about school?
BAH! School, schmool!
When's the last time you ever heard of a legendary hero going to school?!
W- What does that even have to do with...

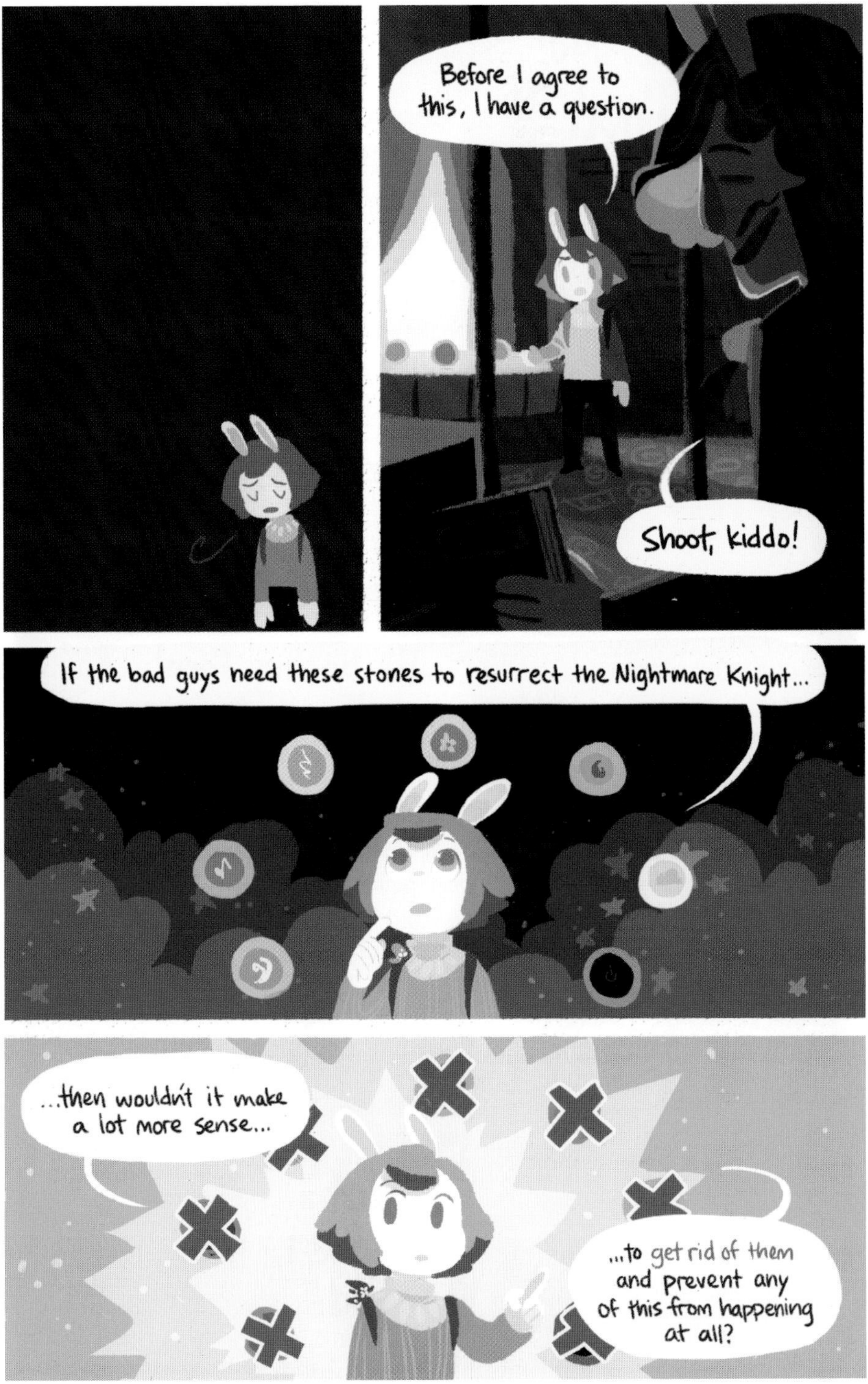
Before I agree to this, I have a question.
Shoot, kiddo!
If the bad guys need these stones to resurrect the Nightmare Knight...
...then wouldn't it make a lot more sense...
...to get rid of them and prevent any of this from happening at all?

What? No! **What?!**

That's
IMPOSSIBLE!

...But they're right there.

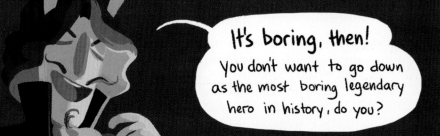

It's boring, then!
You don't want to go down
as the most boring legendary
hero in history, do you?

Well, I don't
really care
about _that_,
Dad.

As long as the
world gets saved
either way...

Not
so fast,
kid!

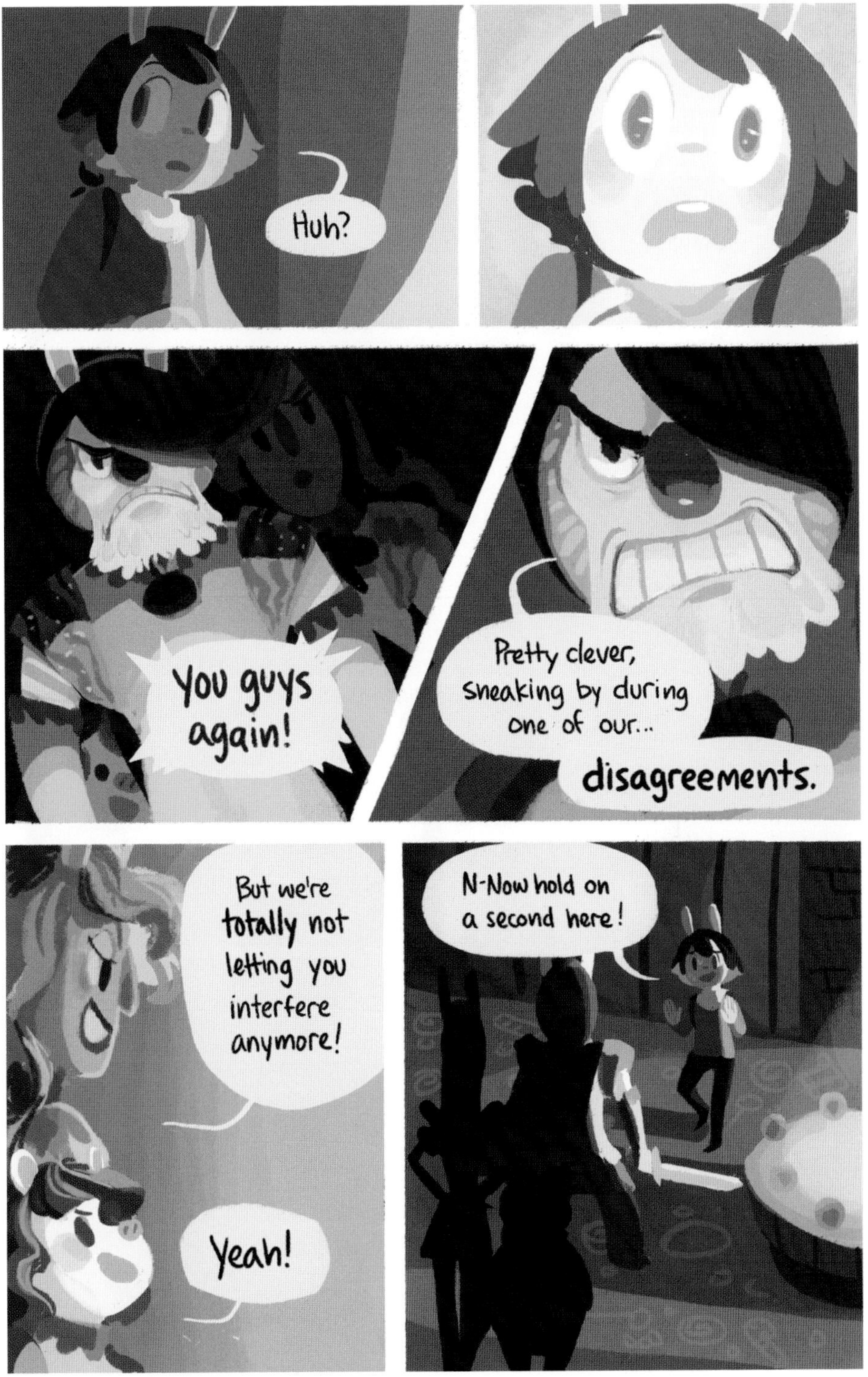
Huh?
You guys again!
Pretty clever, sneaking by during one of our...
disagreements.
But we're totally not letting you interfere anymore!
Yeah!
N-Now hold on a second here!

Uh-oh! This could get really bad!

Why not use some of that ✨magic✨ we're spendin' all that money to send you to school for?

GET PAID

I don't think I like the way you said that at all, **but okay!**

All right, BLT Trio! It's time to

uh

h-hang on a second

rustle rustle

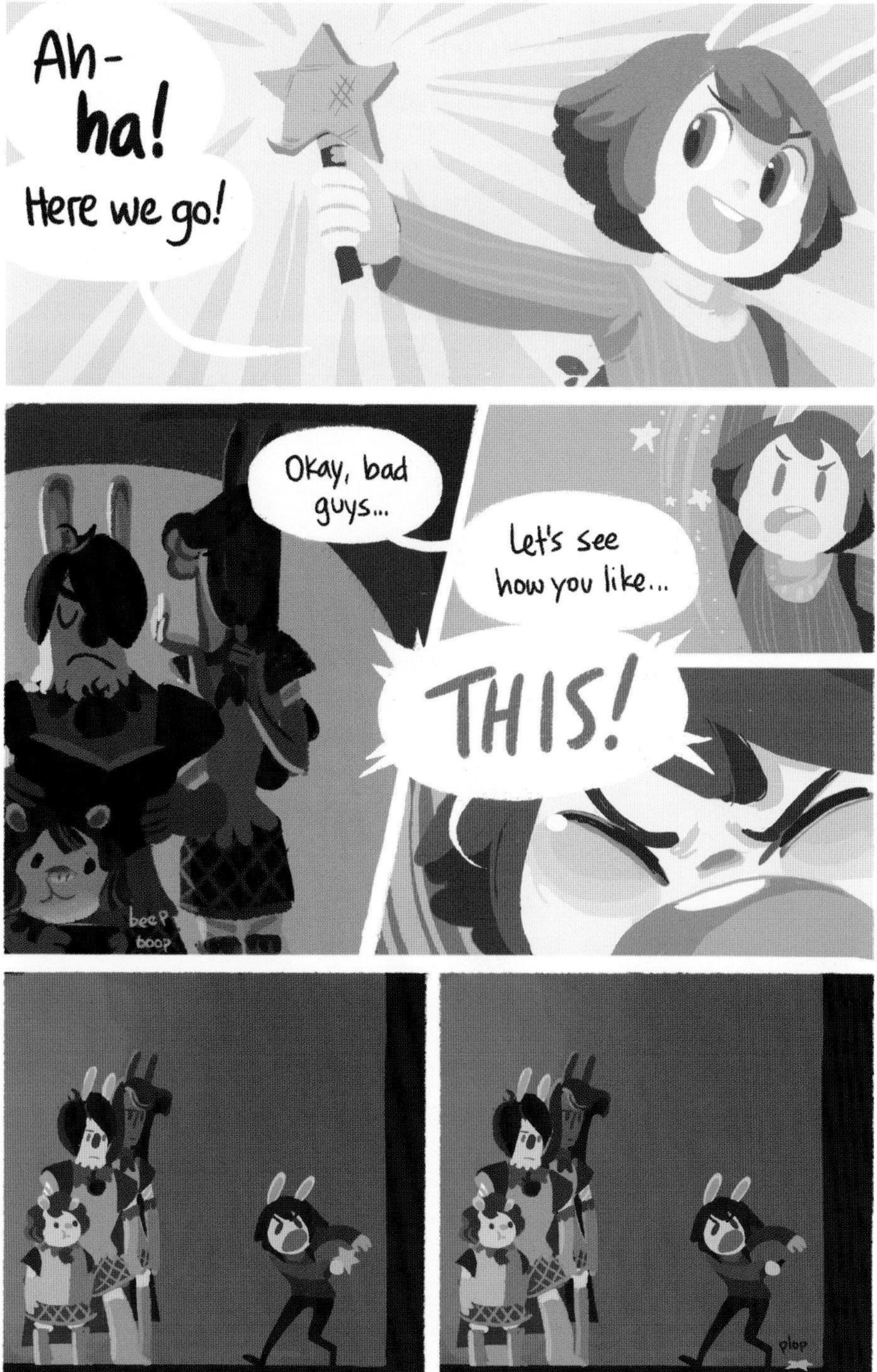
Ah-ha! Here we go!
Okay, bad guys...
beep boop
Let's see how you like...
THIS!
plop

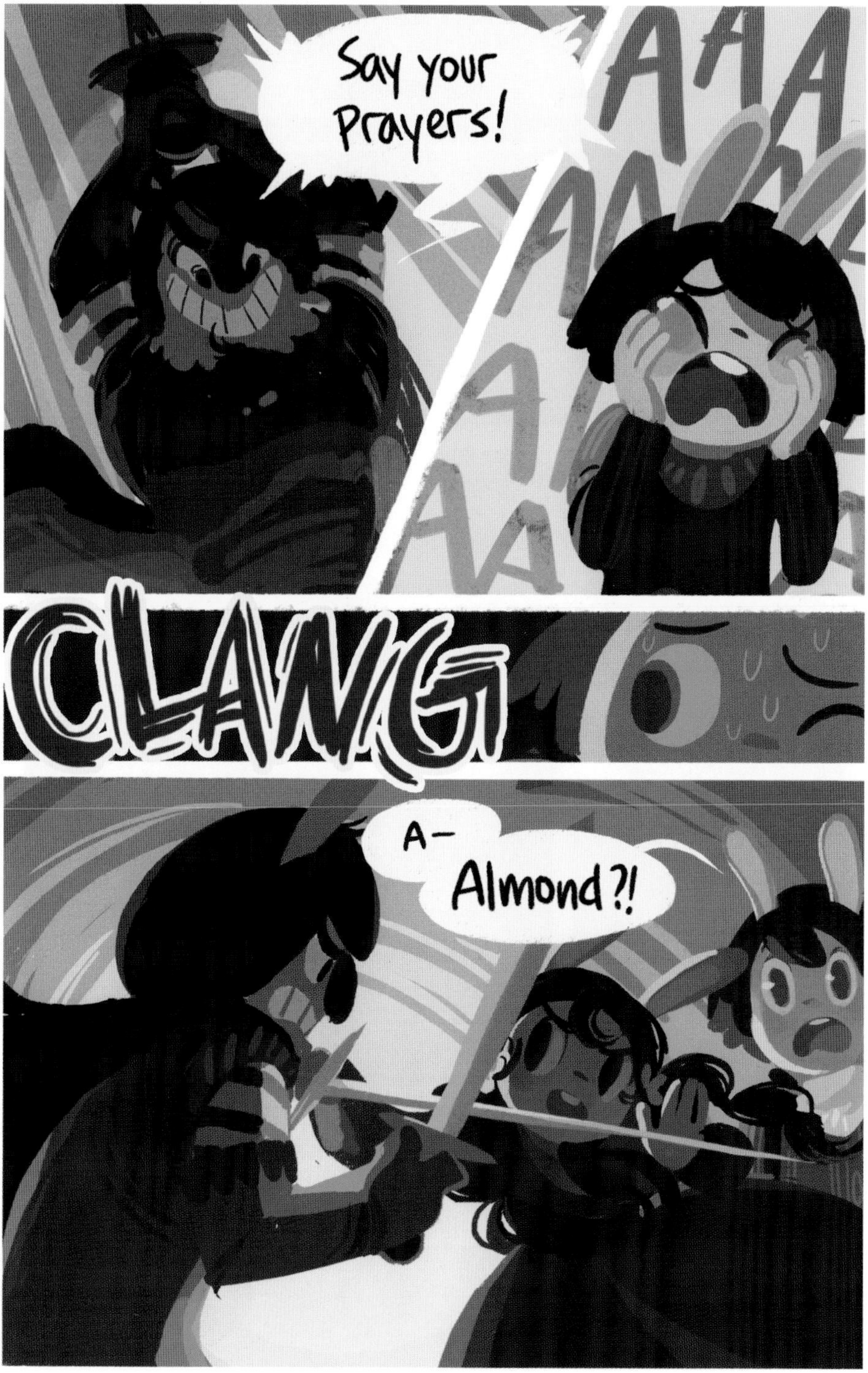
Say your Prayers!
AAAAAAAAAAA
CLANG
A-
Almond?!

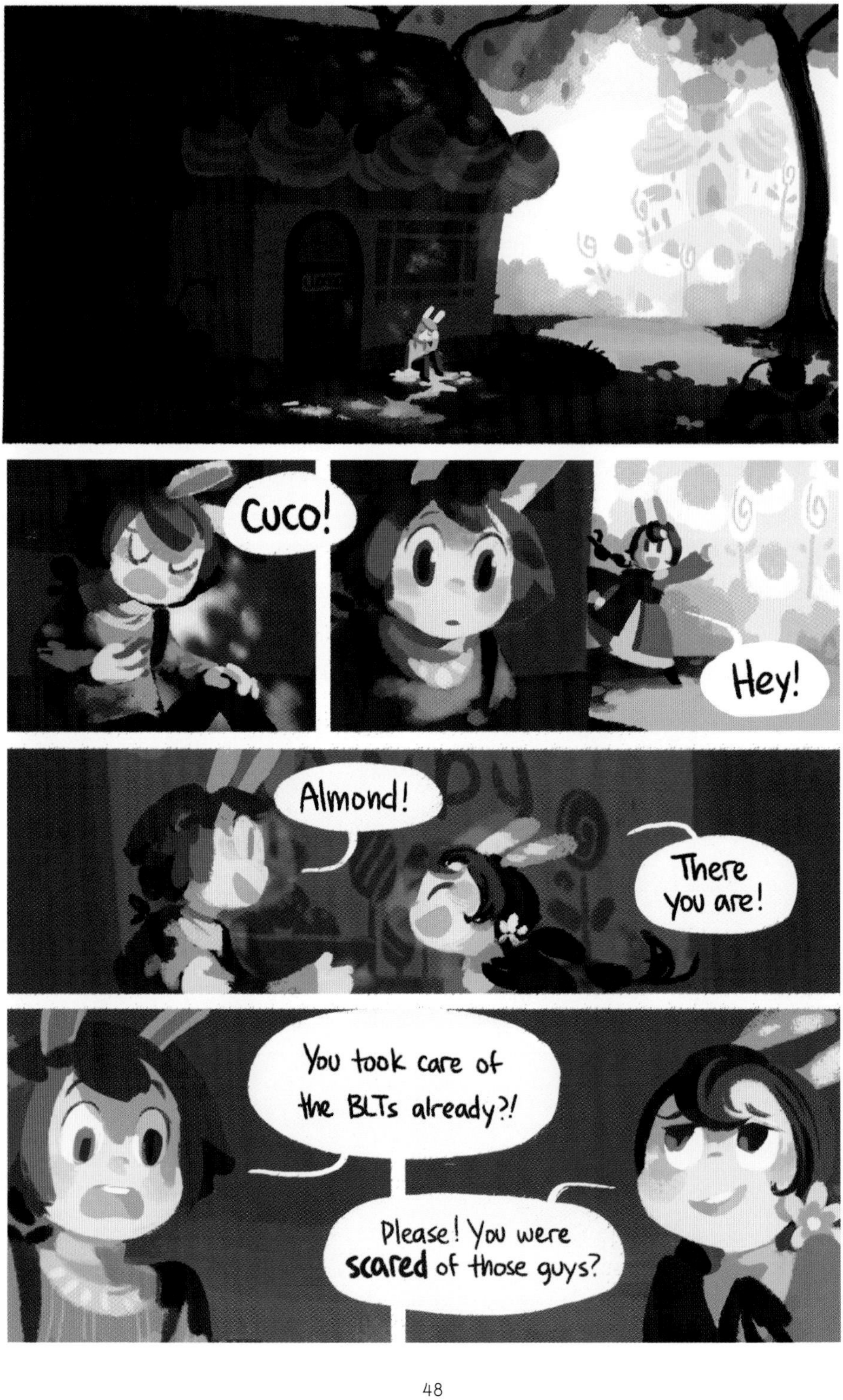
Cuco!
Hey!
Almond!
There you are!
You took care of the BLTs already?!
Please! You were **scared** of those guys?

Instant Replay

I should warn you, kid, I'm not too chivalrous to **hit a girl.**

**In the face.**

**With a sword.**

Scared? It's okay.

I would be too, if I were dealing with the **manliest knight in Caketown.**

If you're not careful, little girl, I just might crush you **like a tomato.**

*wow*

*nice, sir*

So if you're gonna run, now'd be the best **WHY**

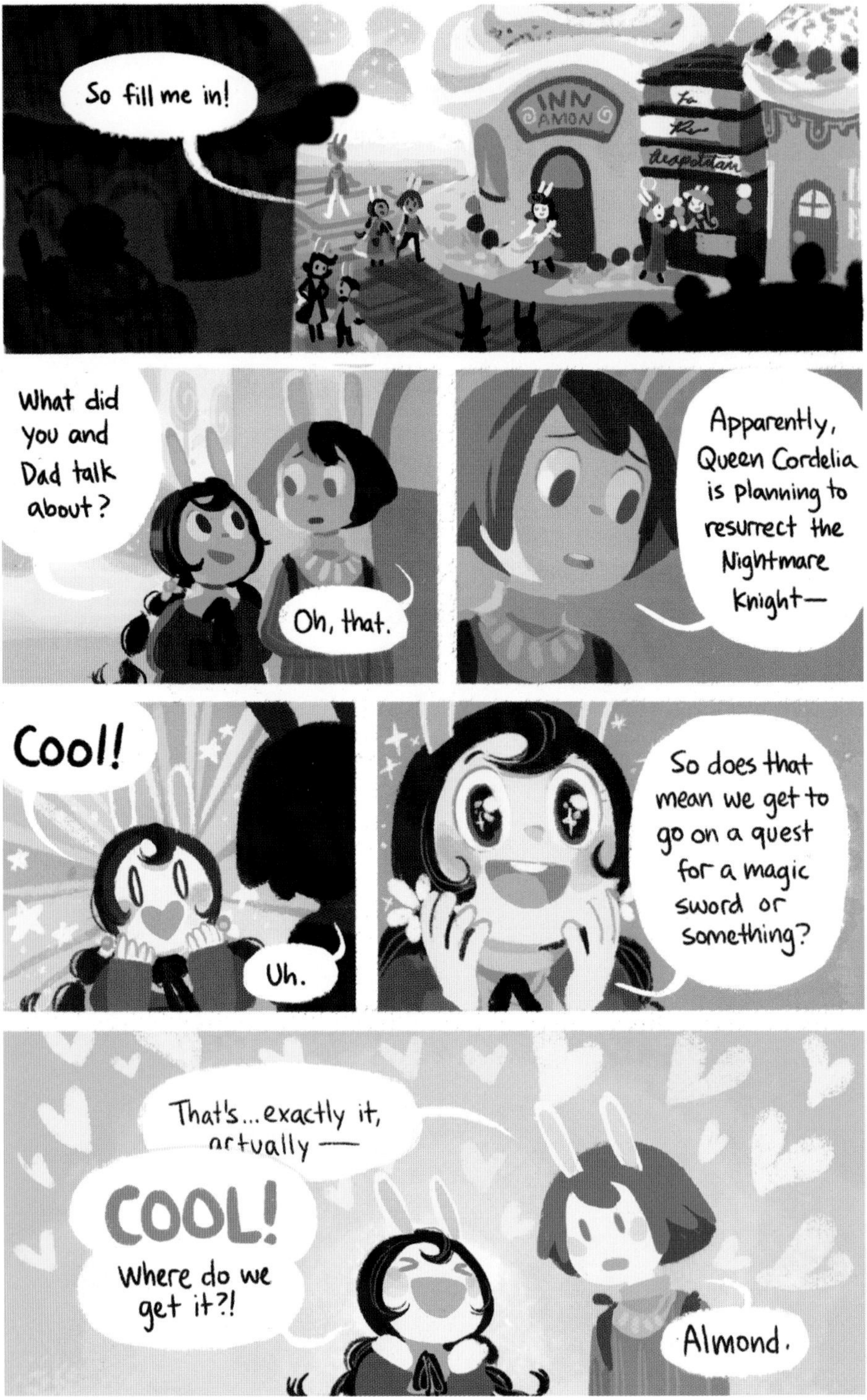
So fill me in!
INN
AMON
What did you and Dad talk about?
Oh, that.
Apparently, Queen Cordelia is planning to resurrect the Nightmare Knight—
Cool!
Uh.
So does that mean we get to go on a quest for a magic sword or something?
That's...exactly it, actually—
COOL! Where do we get it?!
Almond.

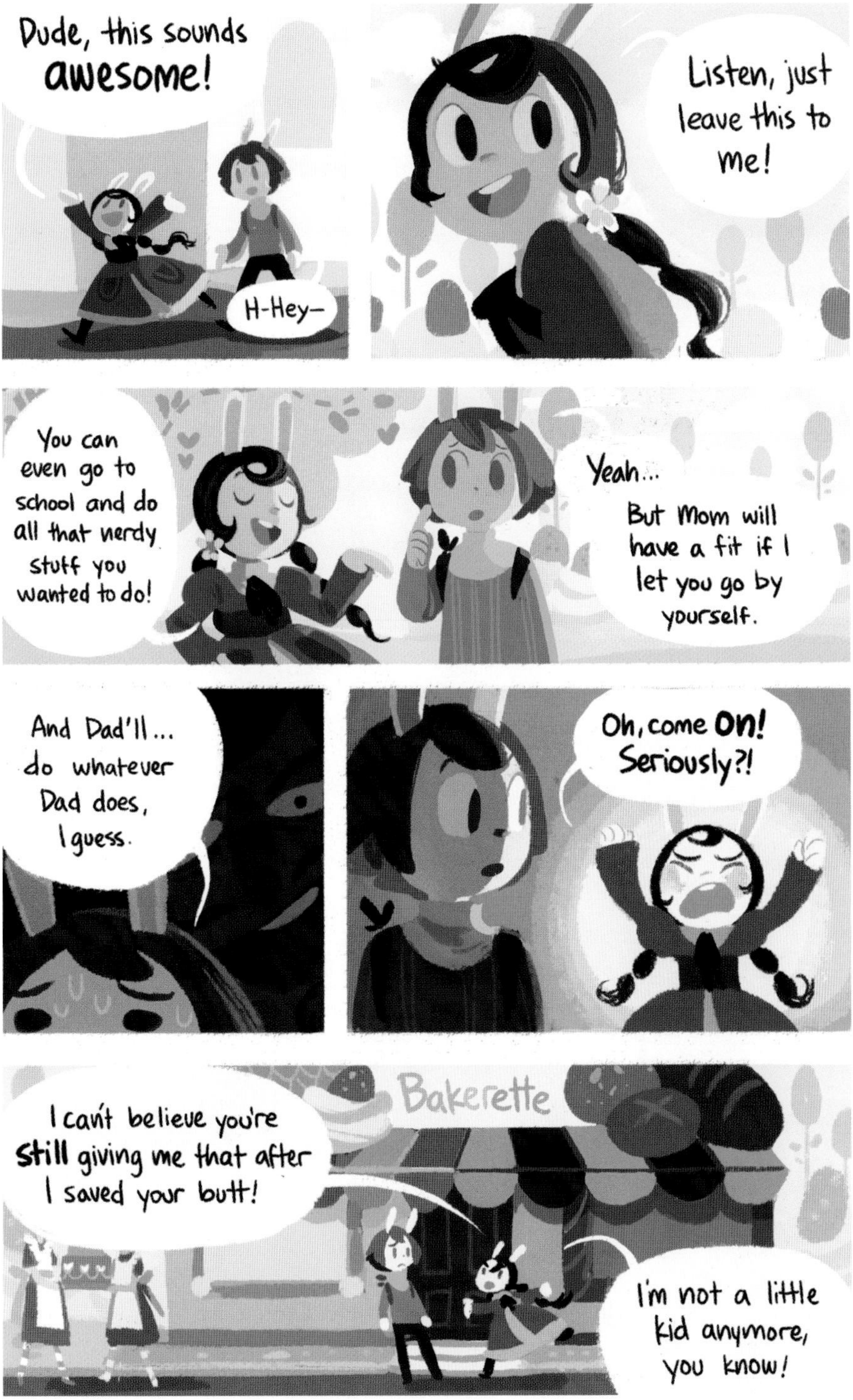
Dude, this sounds **awesome!**
H-Hey—
Listen, just leave this to me!
You can even go to school and do all that nerdy stuff you wanted to do!
Yeah...
But Mom will have a fit if I let you go by yourself.
And Dad'll... do whatever Dad does, I guess.
Oh, come **ON!** Seriously?!
Bakerette
I can't believe you're **still** giving me that after I saved your butt!
I'm not a little kid anymore, you know!

And I can handle way more danger than—

Hey, watch out!

Ow!

CRASH

Way to go, Cuco.

ugh...

Oh!

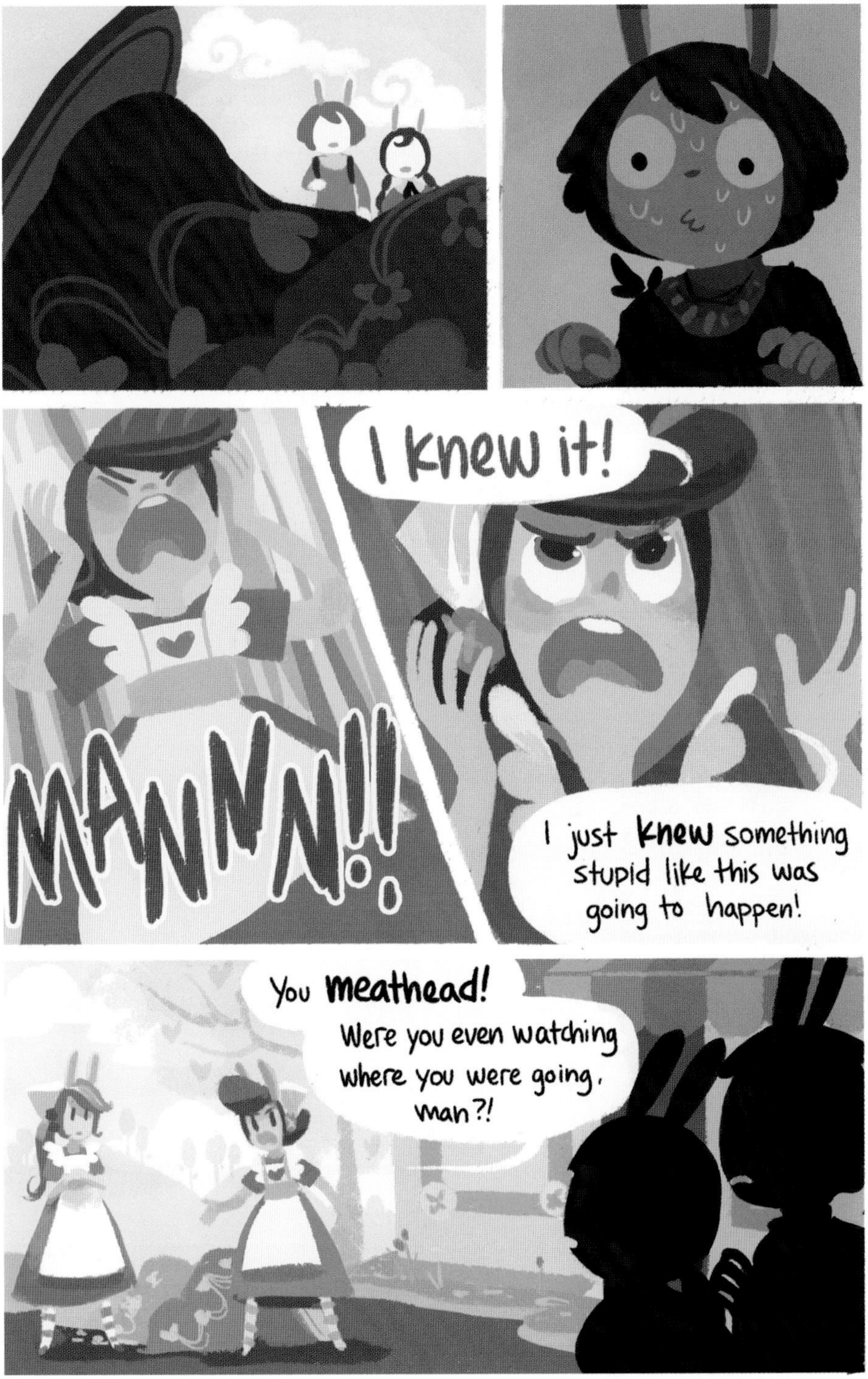
I knew it!
MANNN!!
I just knew something stupid like this was going to happen!
You meathead!
Were you even watching where you were going, man?!

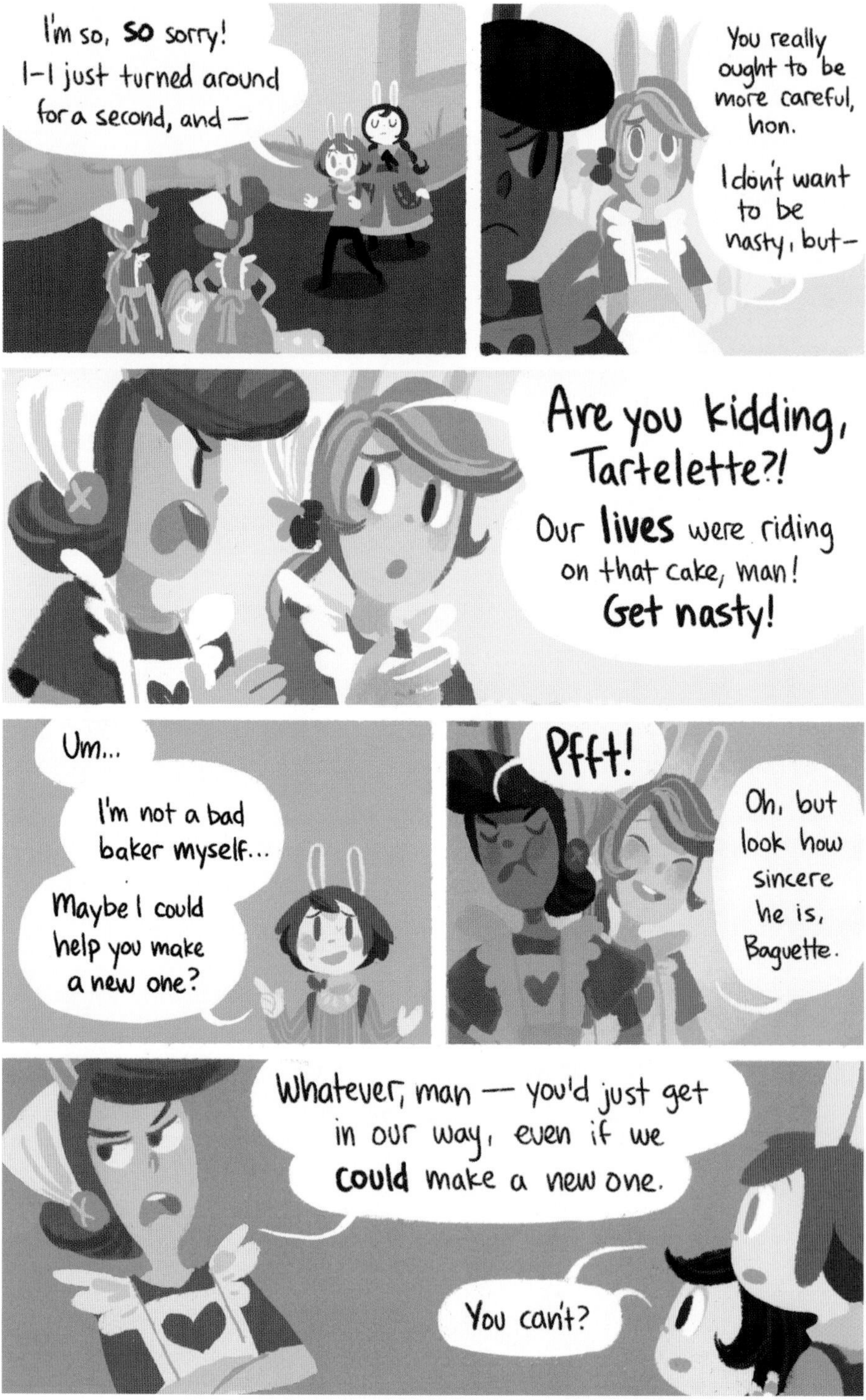
I'm so, **SO** sorry! I-I just turned around for a second, and—
You really ought to be more careful, hon.
I don't want to be nasty, but—
Are you kidding, Tartelette?!
Our **lives** were riding on that cake, man!
**Get nasty!**
Um...
I'm not a bad baker myself...
Maybe I could help you make a new one?
Pfft!
Oh, but look how sincere he is, Baguette.
Whatever, man — you'd just get in our way, even if we **could** make a new one.
You can't?

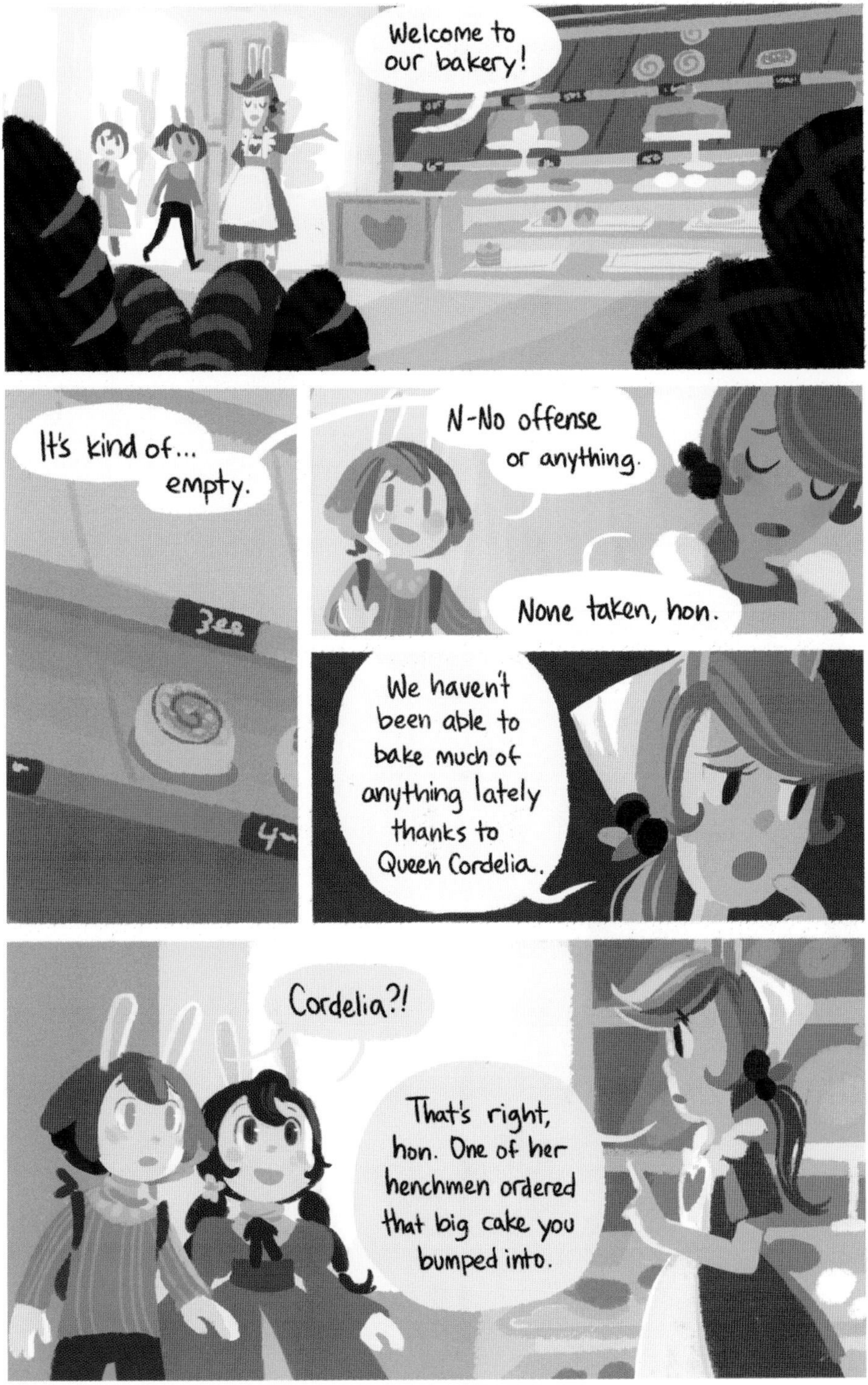
Welcome to our bakery!
It's kind of... empty.
N-No offense or anything.
None taken, hon.
We haven't been able to bake much of anything lately thanks to Queen Cordelia.
Cordelia?!
That's right, hon. One of her henchmen ordered that big cake you bumped into.

It was a loud witch girl who said she'd turn us into stone if we didn't bake a cake for her.

But we're gonna have to close up shop soon, anyway.

See that, man?

It's all we've got left.

SUGAR

Oh. Well, I guess you can't really run a bakery without any sugar.

You can't just get some more?

Look, this is a secret, so don't go telling anybody, all right?

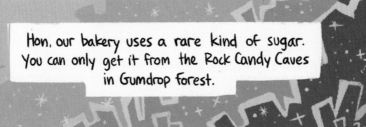

Hon, our bakery uses a rare kind of sugar. You can only get it from the Rock Candy Caves in Gumdrop Forest.

But the forest around the caves is pretty dangerous, so we usually ask knights to collect it for us.

But since Cordelia came, we haven't been able to get any knights to help.

And now that we've used the last of our sugar...

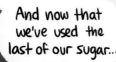

Hey, wait! You said Gumdrop Forest?

We were just going there to see the Oracle!

Yeah! Why don't we get your sugar while we're at it?

Would you really, hon?!

You're life-savers!

# And so:

Hey, um,

why'd you come with us again?

Well, don't take this the wrong way, hon...

It's just, we don't want to take any chances after what happened to the **last** dude we sent here alone.

I think I'll regret asking, but...

What happened to him?

No idea, man! Never heard from him again.

O-Oh.

I bet he got eaten by a monster or something.

Oh, don't say that.

Well, come on, though.

There are monsters here?!

You didn't say all that!

We said it was dangerous, man. What'd you think we meant?

Awesome! I've always wanted to fight a real monster.

I haven't!

L-Listen, are you **sure** you can't just use regular sugar, because I really—

AAAAAAA

What?!

Oof!!

Are...are you a knight?

I-Indeed, milady.

I am called Carrot, a humble servant of His Majesty King Croissant.

WOWWWWWW! I've never met a real, not-evil knight before!

How cool!

So much for that sugar, huh?

A— A thousand pardons!

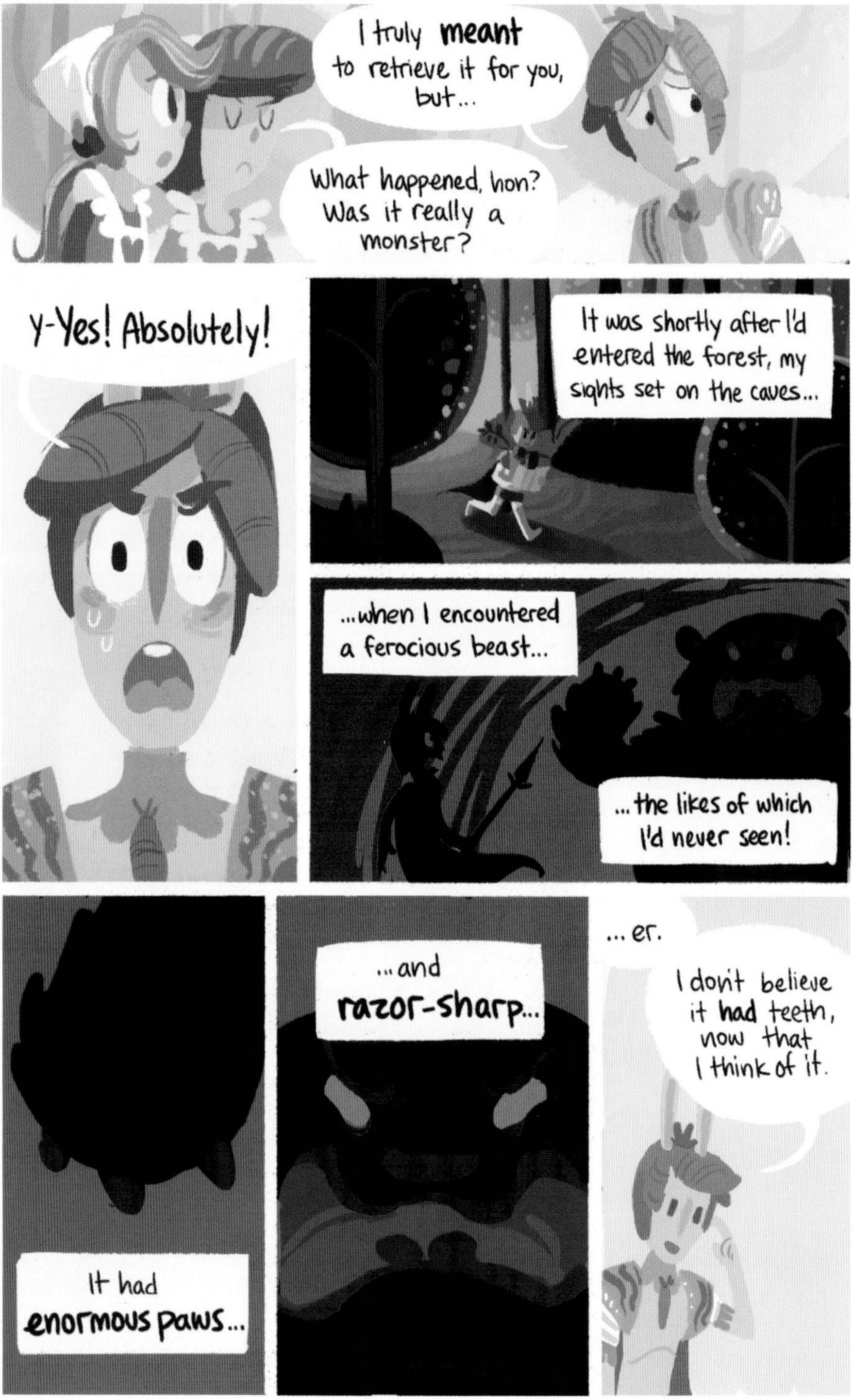
I truly **meant** to retrieve it for you, but...
What happened, hon? Was it really a monster?
Y-Yes! Absolutely!
It was shortly after I'd entered the forest, my sights set on the caves...
...when I encountered a ferocious beast...
...the likes of which I'd never seen!
It had **enormous paws**...
...and **razor-sharp**...
... er.
I don't believe it **had** teeth, now that I think of it.

A-Anyway! I climbed the tallest tree I could find to escape the beast...

And, well... I didn't really think about getting down afterwards.

But I suppose that all worked out in the end, didn't it?

Sure, hon... But what happened to the monster?

GRRRRRRRRRRRRRRRRRRR

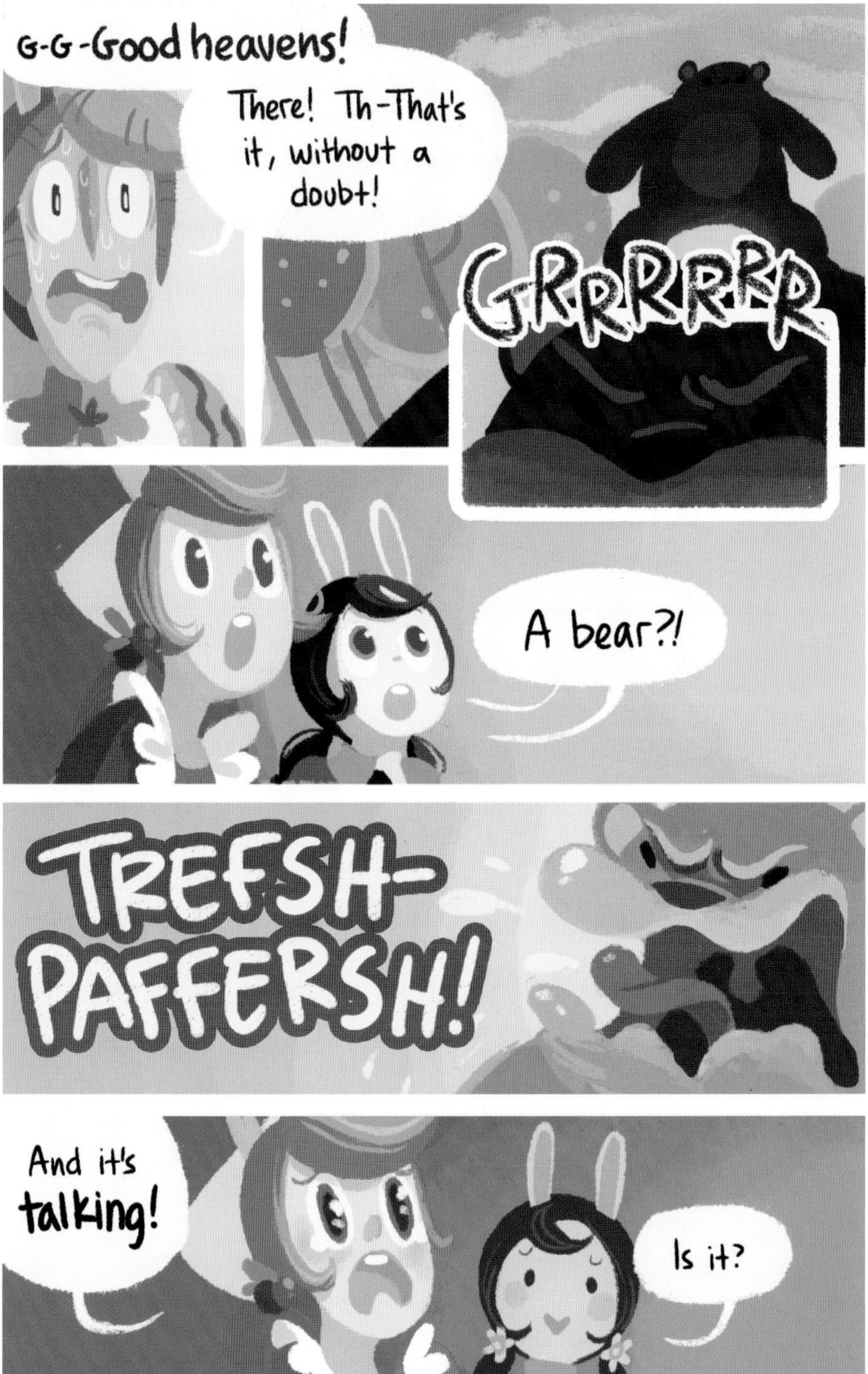
G-G-Good heavens!
There! Th-That's it, without a doubt!
GRRRRR
A bear?!
TREFSH-PAFFERSH!
And it's talking!
Is it?

Hey, wait...

I've read about this before!

It's Grizzlygum!

Grizzly-**what?**

Grizzly GUM!

Legends say he's the toothless guardian of Gumdrop Forest!

Thatsh right!

And I'm **ffffthick** offavin' ta keep you nosy kidsh oudda here! Alwaysh comin' in an' tramplin' all over the flowers! n' fthcarin' the birdsh ... you troublemakin' good-fe ... deanin' up afte ... yer ... ll the Oracle about ...

66

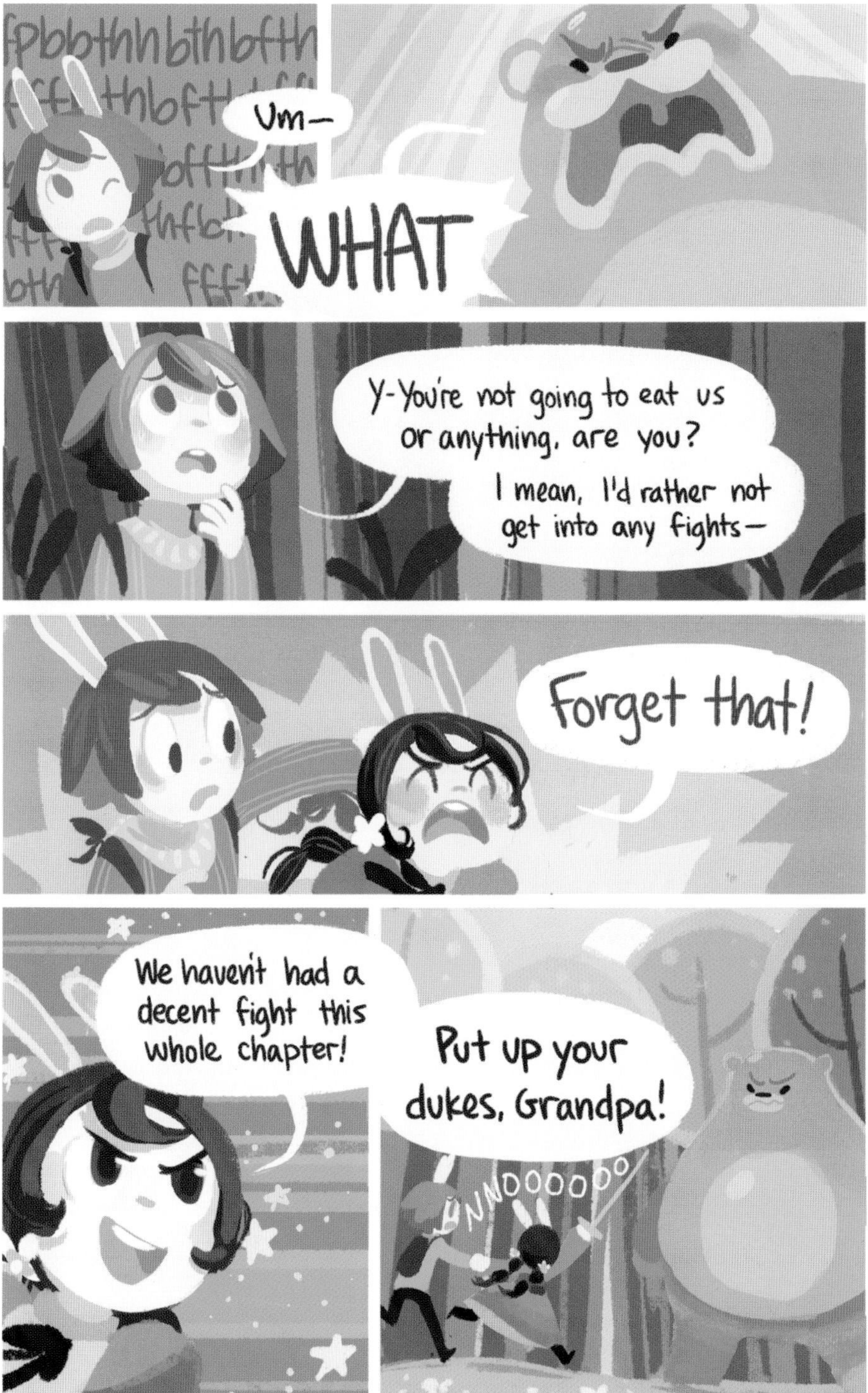

fpbbthhbthbfth
Um—
WHAT
Y-You're not going to eat us or anything, are you?
I mean, I'd rather not get into any fights—
Forget that!
We haven't had a decent fight this whole chapter!
Put up your dukes, Grandpa!
NNOOOOOO

Fight...?

HAR! I don't wanna fight you kidsh!

But... didn't you attack Sir Carrot?

Attack 'im?!

NO! I don't hurt people, jush want 'em to shtay oudda where they don't belong!

I jush wanted to give 'im a lil' talk, ish all!

Ah! Well, you see, I never said he **attacked** me, per se...

Are you for real?

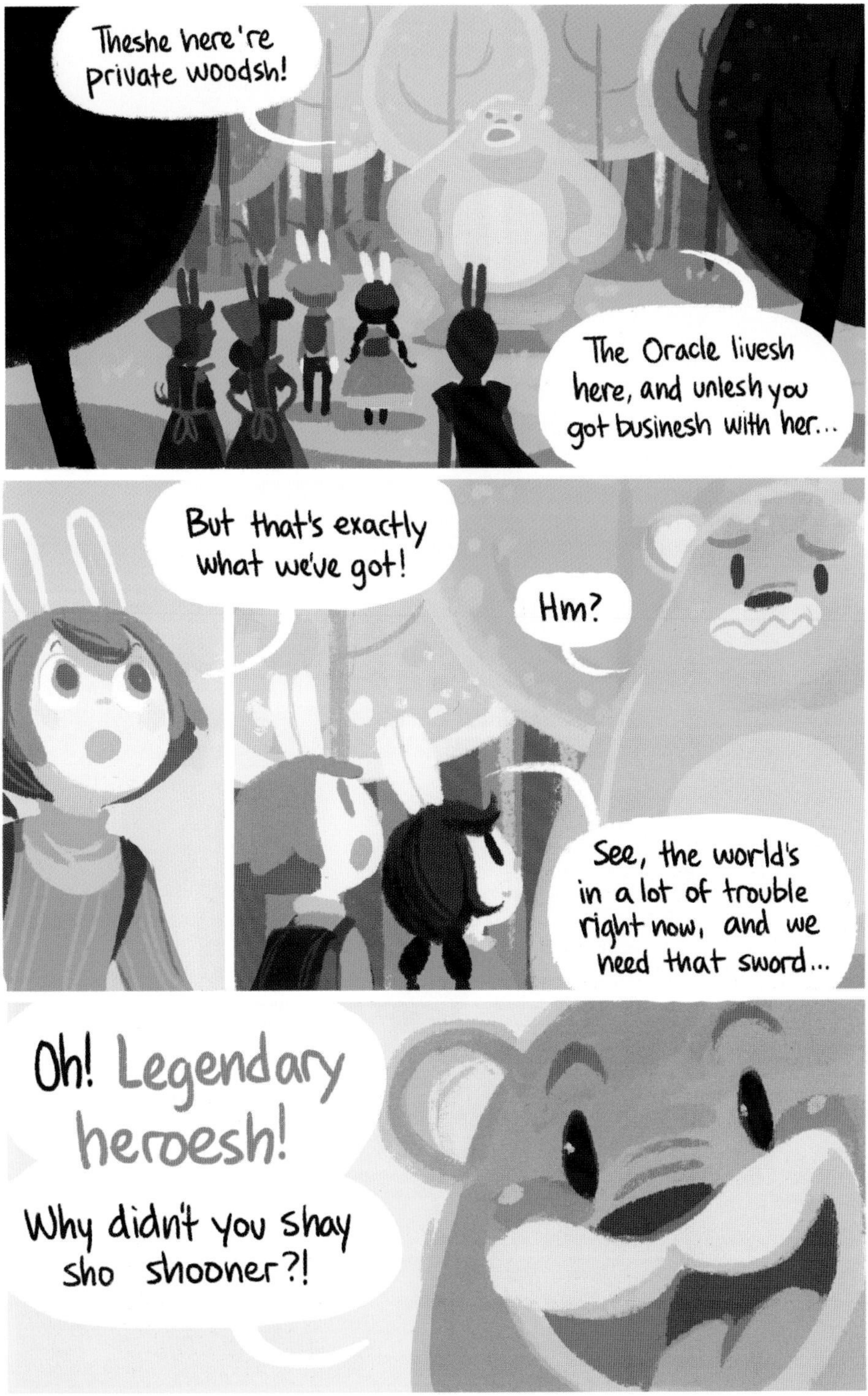
Theshe here're private woodsh!
The Oracle livesh here, and unlesh you got businesh with her...
But that's exactly what we've got!
Hm?
See, the world's in a lot of trouble right now, and we need that sword...
Oh! Legendary heroesh!
Why didn't you shay sho shooner?!

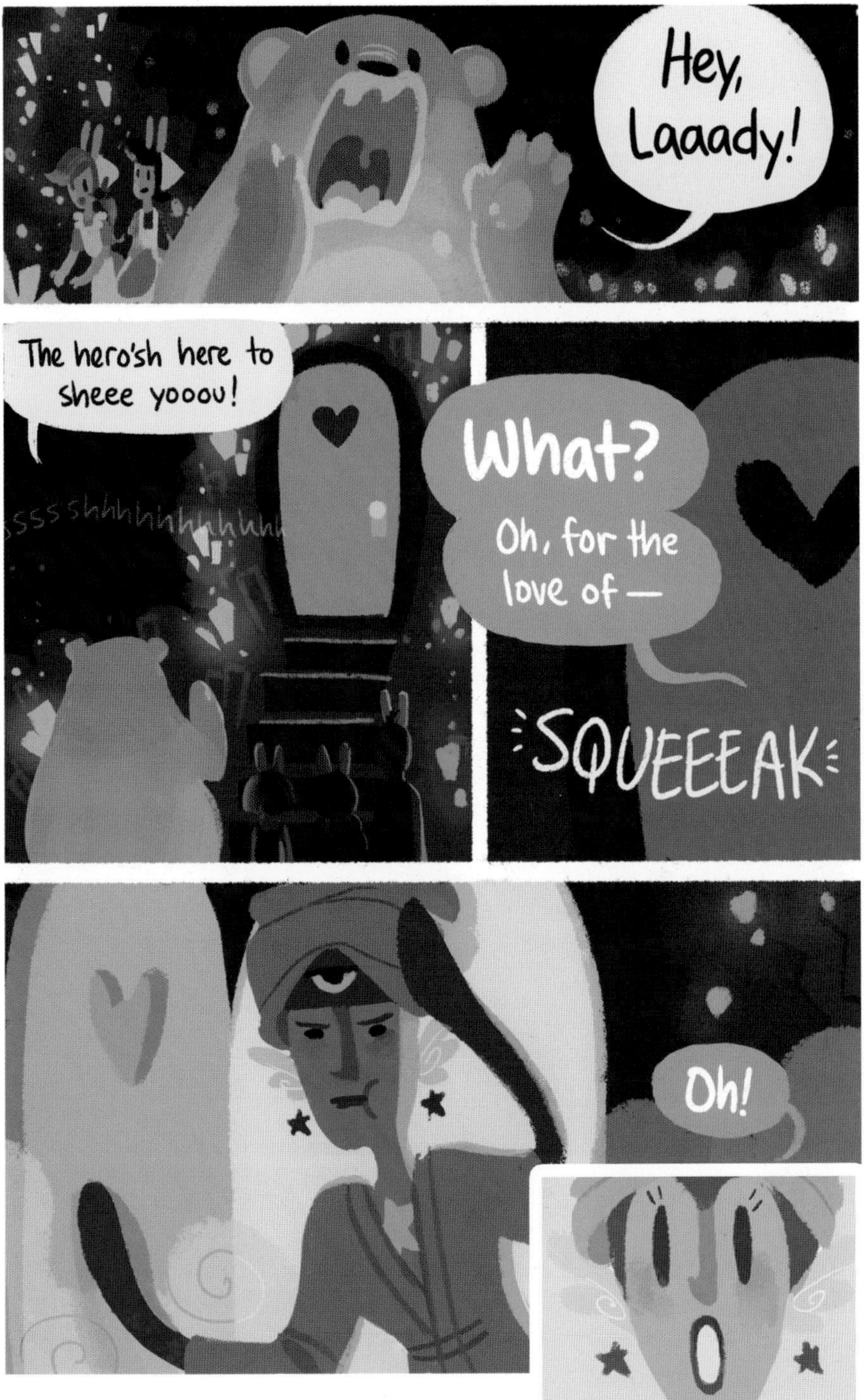

Hey, Laaady!
The hero'sh here to sheee yooou!
ssssshhhhhhhhhhhh
What?
Oh, for the love of—
SQUEEEAK
Oh!

W-What are you talking about? That isn't even possible!

Grizzlygum, is this the truth?

Hmm...

I don't rememmer anybody elsh comin' in today, Lady.

You shure?

...What?

But then... Who did I give the Dream Sword to?

Awwww, forgot me already?!

73

But — **WHAT?!** We don't even look anything alike!

Or **sound** anything alike! Or— or anything anything alike!

Oh, for goodness' sake, it's the red hair.

How am I supposed to tell all you bunny people apart, anyway?

But isn't this your **job?!**

**Well, excuse you!** For your information, sweetheart, I have a very busy schedule.

I don't have time to spend interrogating every "legendary hero" who walks in here!

But—

But that's just **stupid!**

Wasn't that sword supposed to stop the Nightmare Knight?

Aw, this ol' thing?

If y'all want this so bad...

...then come 'n get it!

EMERGENCY EXIT

SLAM!!

H- Hey!

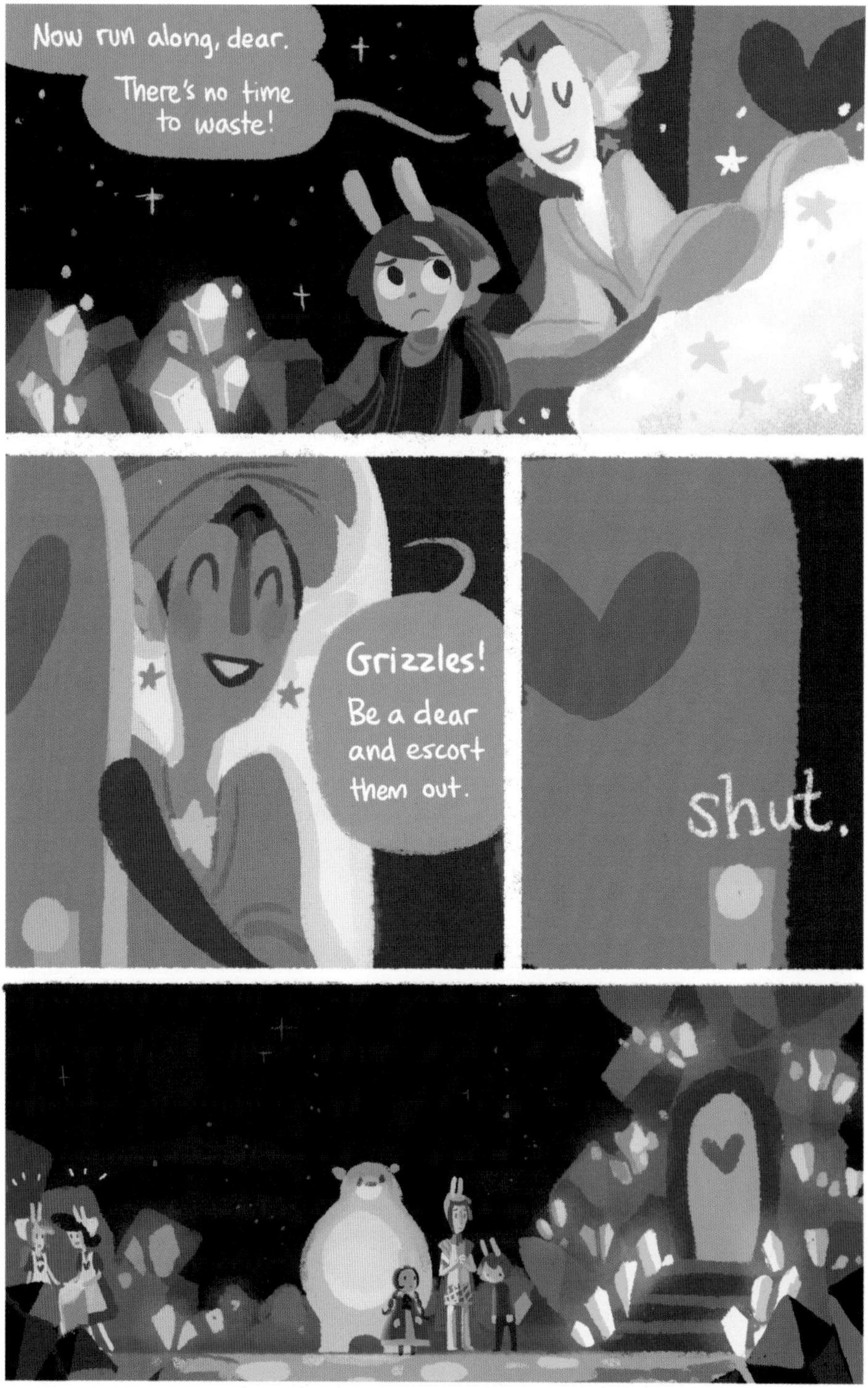
Now run along, dear.
There's no time to waste!
Grizzles! Be a dear and escort them out.
shut.

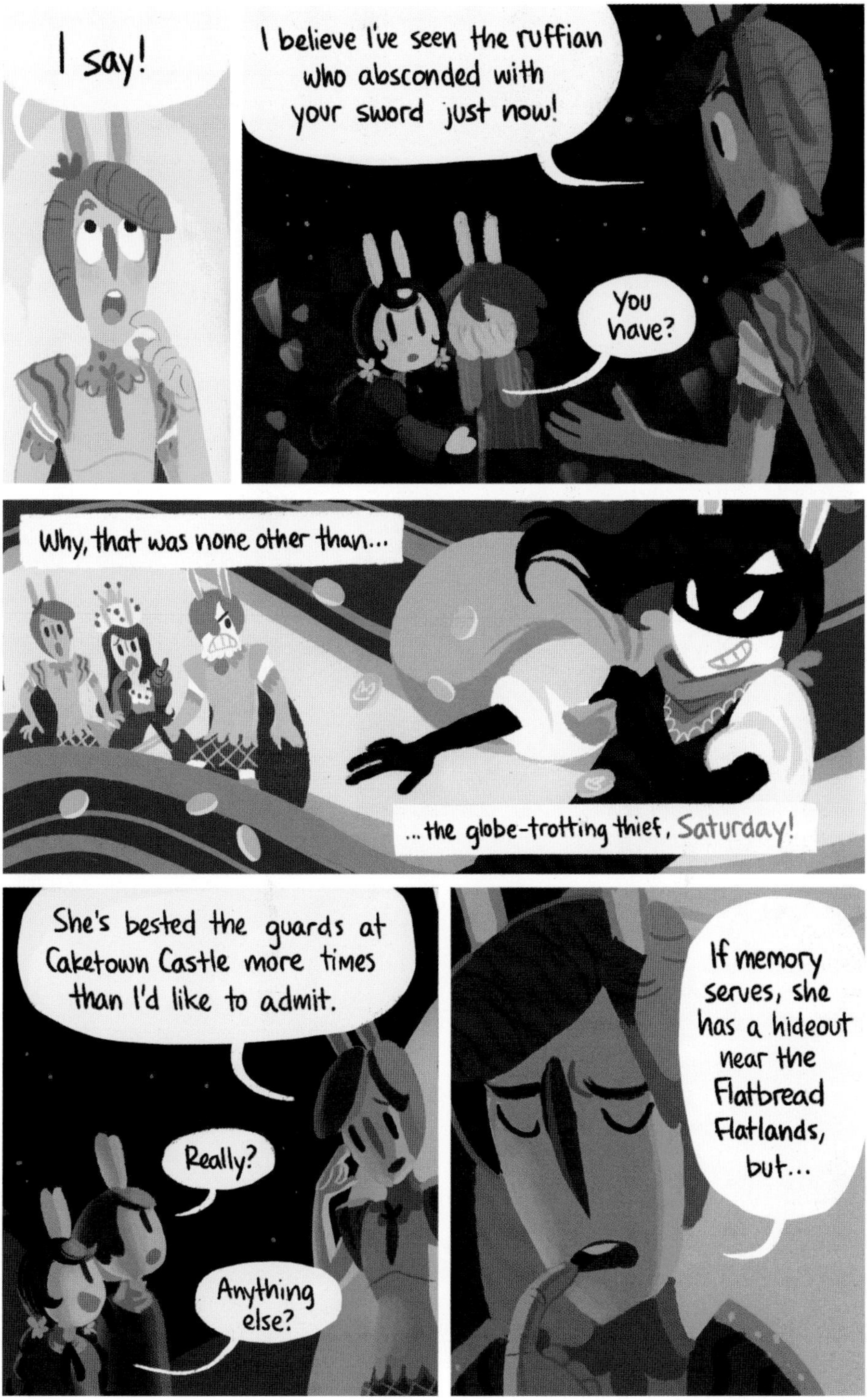
I say!
I believe I've seen the ruffian who absconded with your sword just now!
You have?
Why, that was none other than...
...the globe-trotting thief, Saturday!
She's bested the guards at Caketown Castle more times than I'd like to admit.
Really?
Anything else?
If memory serves, she has a hideout near the Flatbread Flatlands, but...

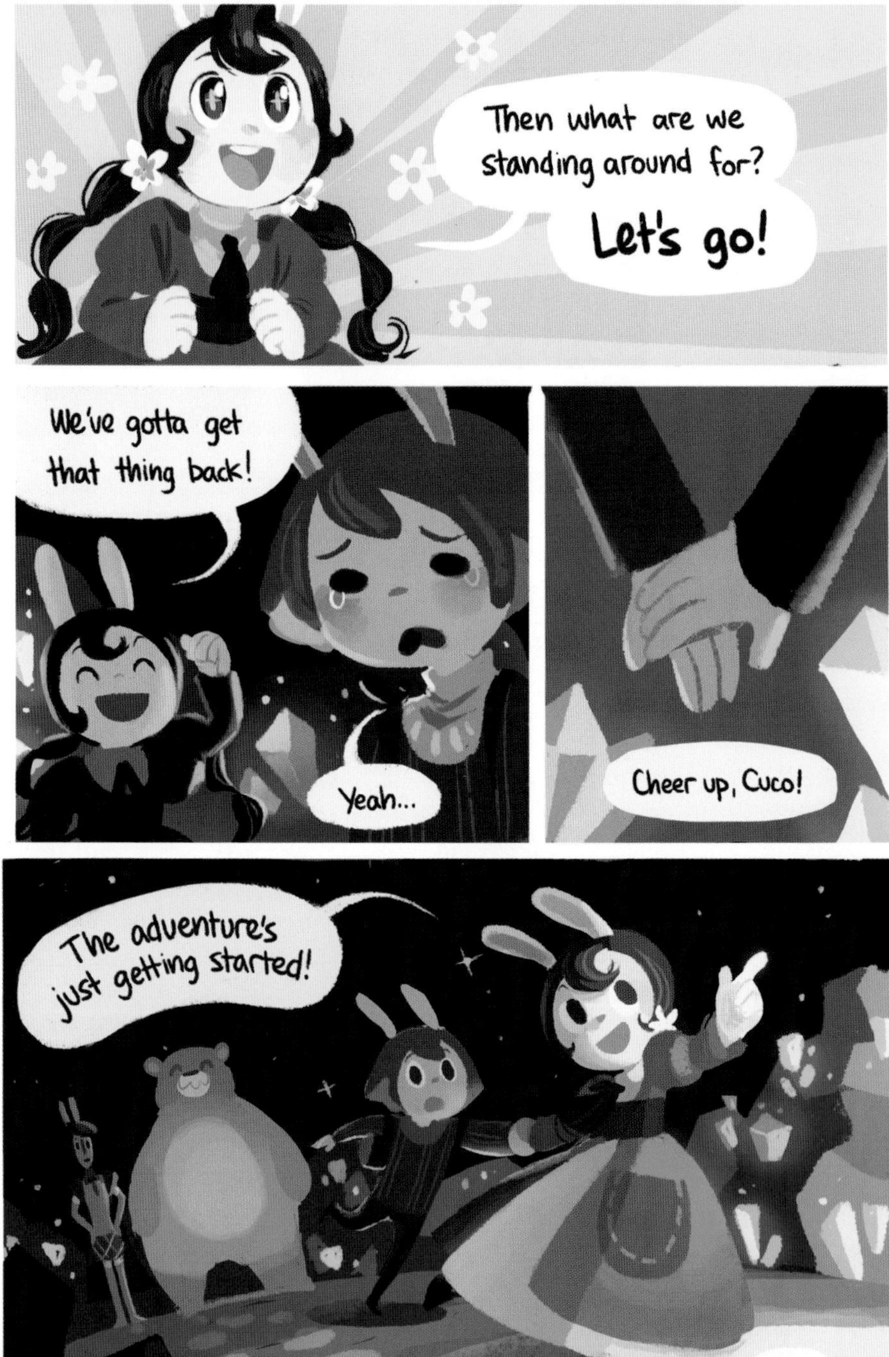
Then what are we standing around for?
Let's go!
We've gotta get that thing back!
Yeah...
Cheer up, Cuco!
The adventure's just getting started!

# Cucumber

Atk ⭐⭐
Def ⭐⭐⭐
Sp ⭐⭐⭐⭐

⚙ "borrowed" wand
📖 encyclopedia
✉ acceptance letter

Cucumber is an aspiring wizard who **should** currently be enrolled in the magic school of his dreams, but ~~the return of an ancient evil~~ his weird, pushy dad has forced him into the role of a legendary hero instead. While he may lack a sense of adventure, "Cuco" has both a kind heart and a good head on his shoulders.

# Almond

Atk ⭐⭐⭐⭐⭐
Def ⭐⭐
Sp ⭐⭐

 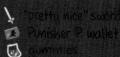

🗡 "pretty nice" sword
👛 Punisher P. wallet
🍬 gummies

With her top-notch swordsmanship and an endless supply of sass, Almond is way more into this hero thing than her big bro. So into it, in fact, that she aids in the resurrection of an ancient lord of darkness because the alternative would be "boring."

She'll make a fine knight someday.

# The Dream Oracle

Atk ⭐
Def ⭐⭐⭐
Sp ⭐⭐⭐⭐⭐

👁 all-seeing eye
🪄 all-seeing wand
🧥 cute bathrobe

The world of Dreamside is always protected under the watchful eyes of the Oracle... whenever she can manage to tear them away from her favorite TV shows. Sure, it was thanks to her guidance that the Nightmare Knight was first sealed away, but since then, she seems to have perfected the art of avoiding responsibility. It's almost impressive.

# Lord Cabbage

Atk ⭐
Def ⭐
Jerk ⭐⭐⭐⭐⭐+

✨ money
📦 more money
💰 most money

Caketown's resident weird, pushy dad seems to value making his son's life miserable over everything else (except money). It's very possible that beneath his jerkface exterior lies the soul of a caring parent who wants only the best for his kids...

...Yeah, never mind.

# Sir Tomato

Atk ★★★★★    🗡 manly sword
Def ★★★       🧴 cloying cologne
Sp ★          📖 book of one-liners

As the self-proclaimed "manliest knight in Caketown," Tomato spends his time picking fights with children and tirelessly hitting on a princess who couldn't be less interested in him. His bumbling sidekicks are always around to make him look, uh... "good."

# Dame Lettuce

Atk ★★★     🗡 delicate sword
Def ★★      💄 favorite lipstick
Sp ★★★★   📔 secret diary

Ditzy Dame Lettuce has always been Sir Tomato's number one fan, and she might just be, like, literally the **ONLY** woman who can stand to be around him. The truth is that she's got a pretty major crush on him, but unfortunately (?) for her, he's too clueless to notice.

# Sir Bacon

Atk ⭐
Def ⭐
Sp ⭐

🗡 wooden sword
🍭 lollipop
📦 *Food on Food* DVDs

Nah.

# Saturday

Atk ⭐⭐⭐
Def ⭐⭐
Sp ⭐⭐⭐⭐

everybody
else's stuff

Little is known about this energetic master thief, but she sure knows a thing or two about being a complete nuisance. And come on — that can't be her **real** name, can it?

# CHAPTER O

The Nightmare Knight's Return

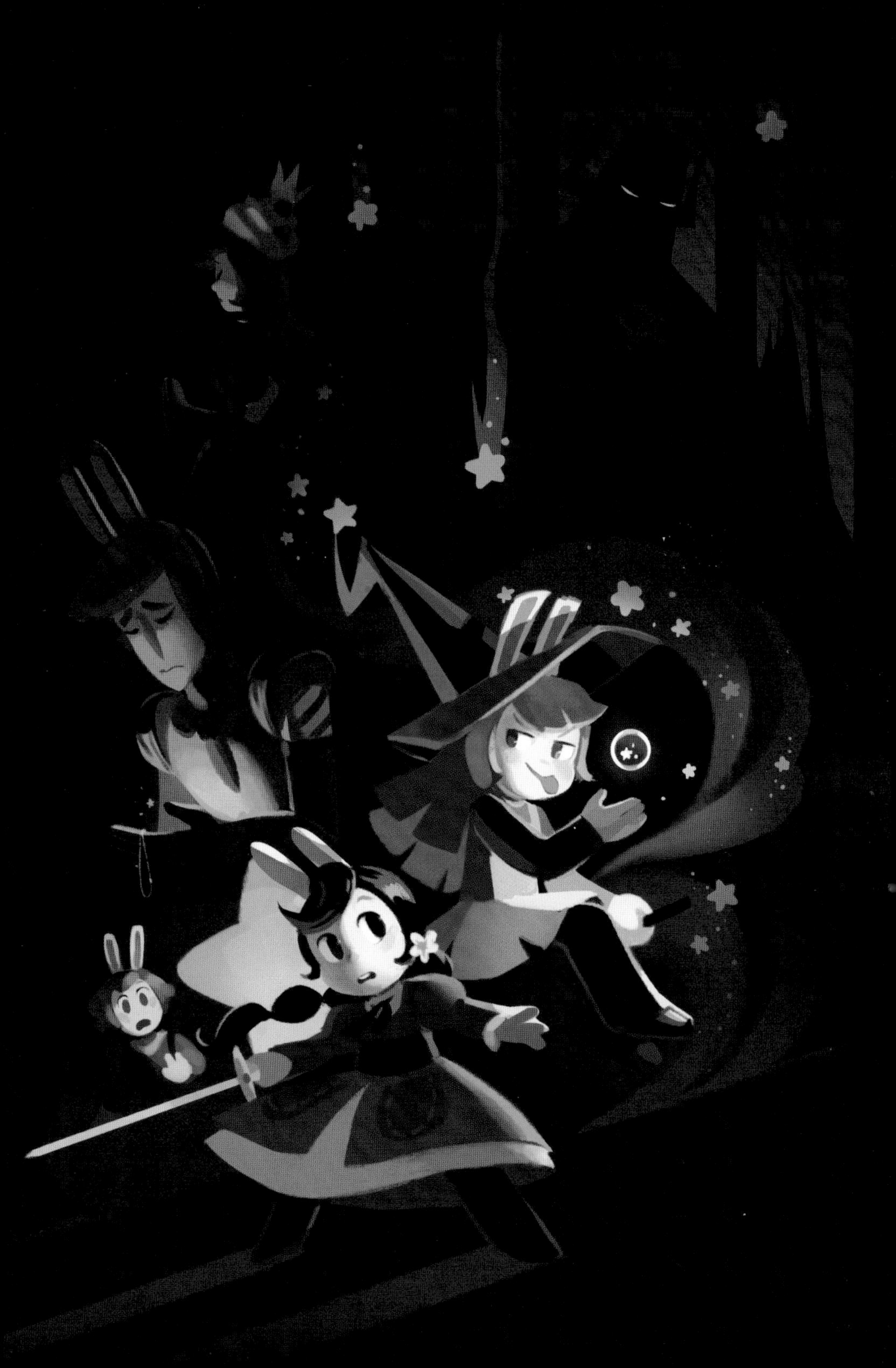

*caw*

*caw*

Thanks for escorting us, hon!

No problem!

Yeah! It was the least we could do to make up for your cake.

You can say that again, man.

heh.

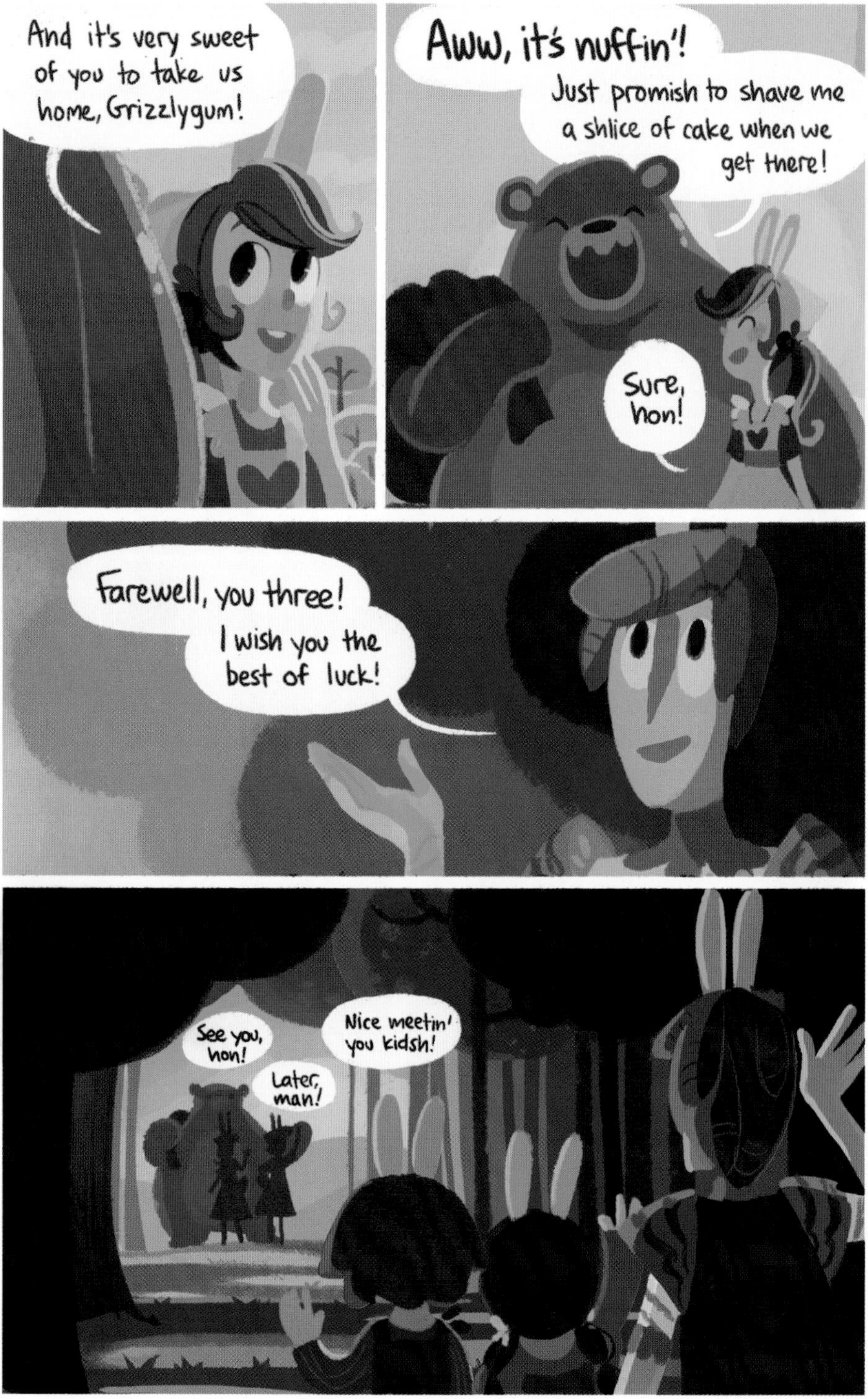

And it's very sweet of you to take us home, Grizzlygum!
Aww, it's nuffin'!
Just promish to shave me a shlice of cake when we get there!
Sure, hon!
Farewell, you three!
I wish you the best of luck!
See you, hon!
Nice meetin' you kidsh!
Later, man!

So... you're really going to come with us?

But of course!

The kingdom is in danger!

I will not stand idly by as injustice prevails!

And, well, since Cordelia came, I havent had a bunna hunna hum

You got kicked out?

A-Ahem!

W-Well, I, er, h-hesitate to say...

...yes.

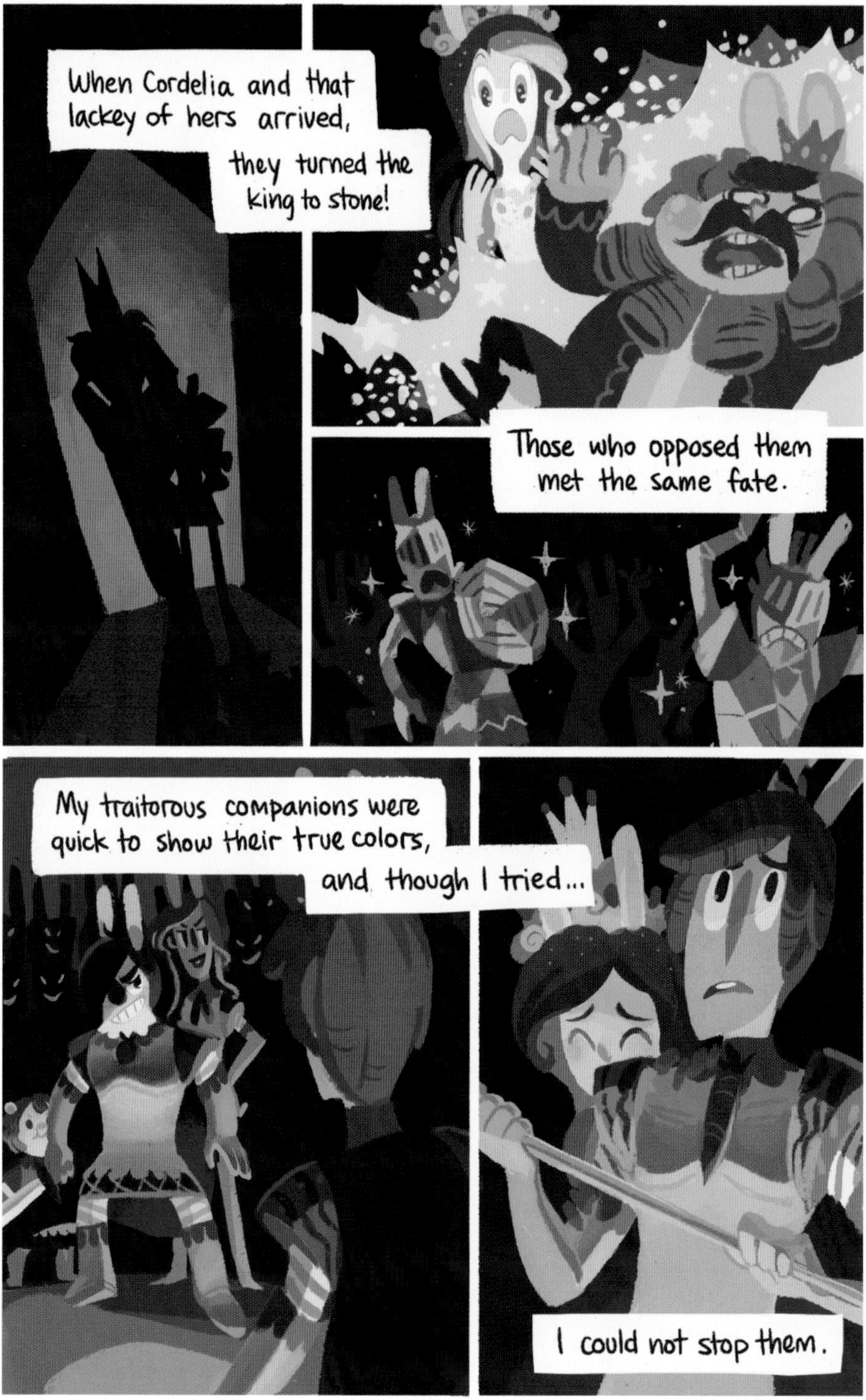
When Cordelia and that lackey of hers arrived,
they turned the king to stone!
Those who opposed them met the same fate.
My traitorous companions were quick to show their true colors,
and though I tried...
I could not stop them.

95

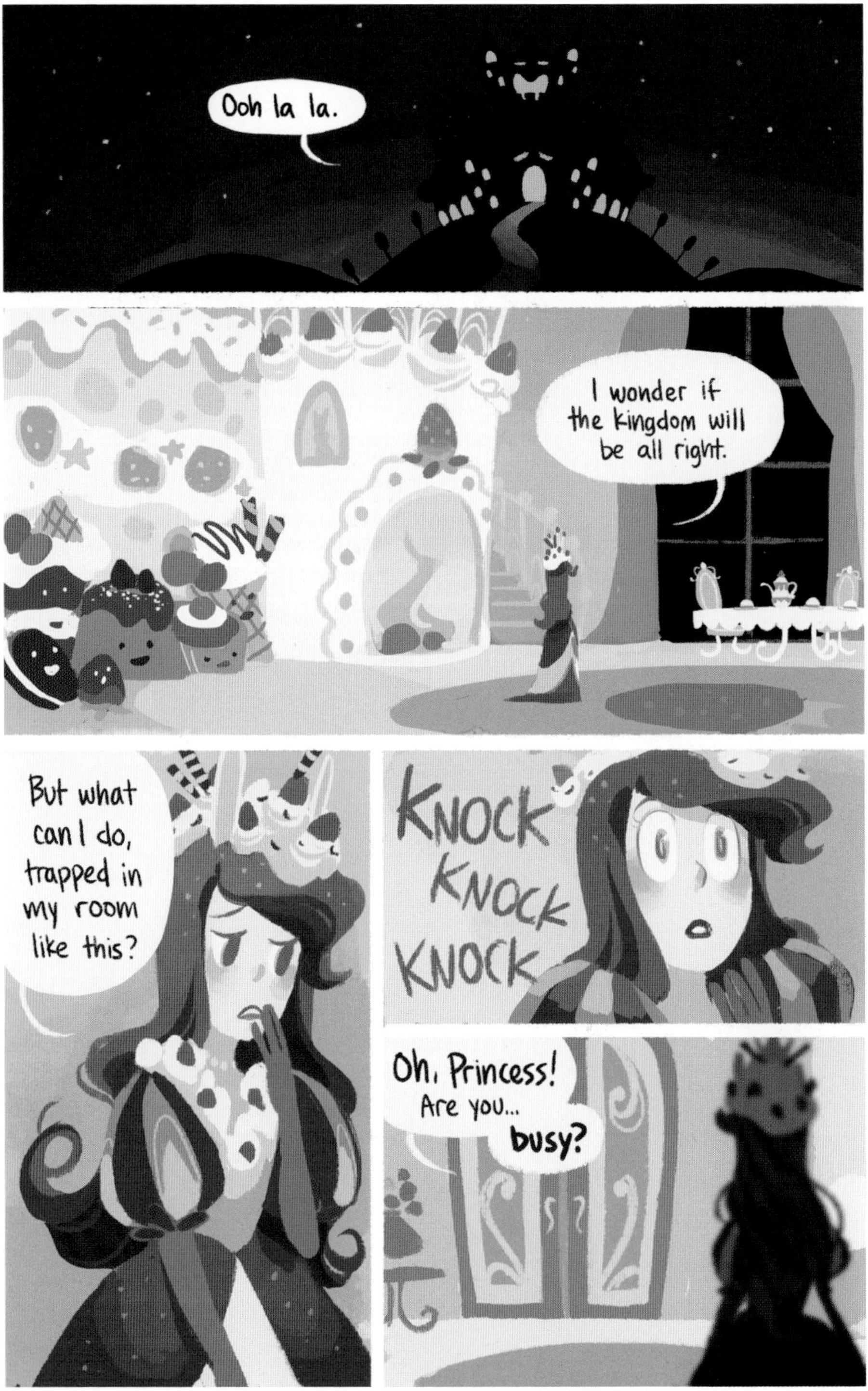
Ooh la la.
I wonder if the kingdom will be all right.
But what can I do, trapped in my room like this?
KNOCK
KNOCK
KNOCK
Oh, Princess!
Are you...
busy?

Hmph! Per'aps when you let me see my papa, I will be less cruel!

GASP

Ohmygosh, **rude!!**

It's, like, a total honor that Sir Tomato is even, like, **talking** to you!

If I ever got that kind of attention from him, I—

chomp chomp

CHOMP chomp smack mmph

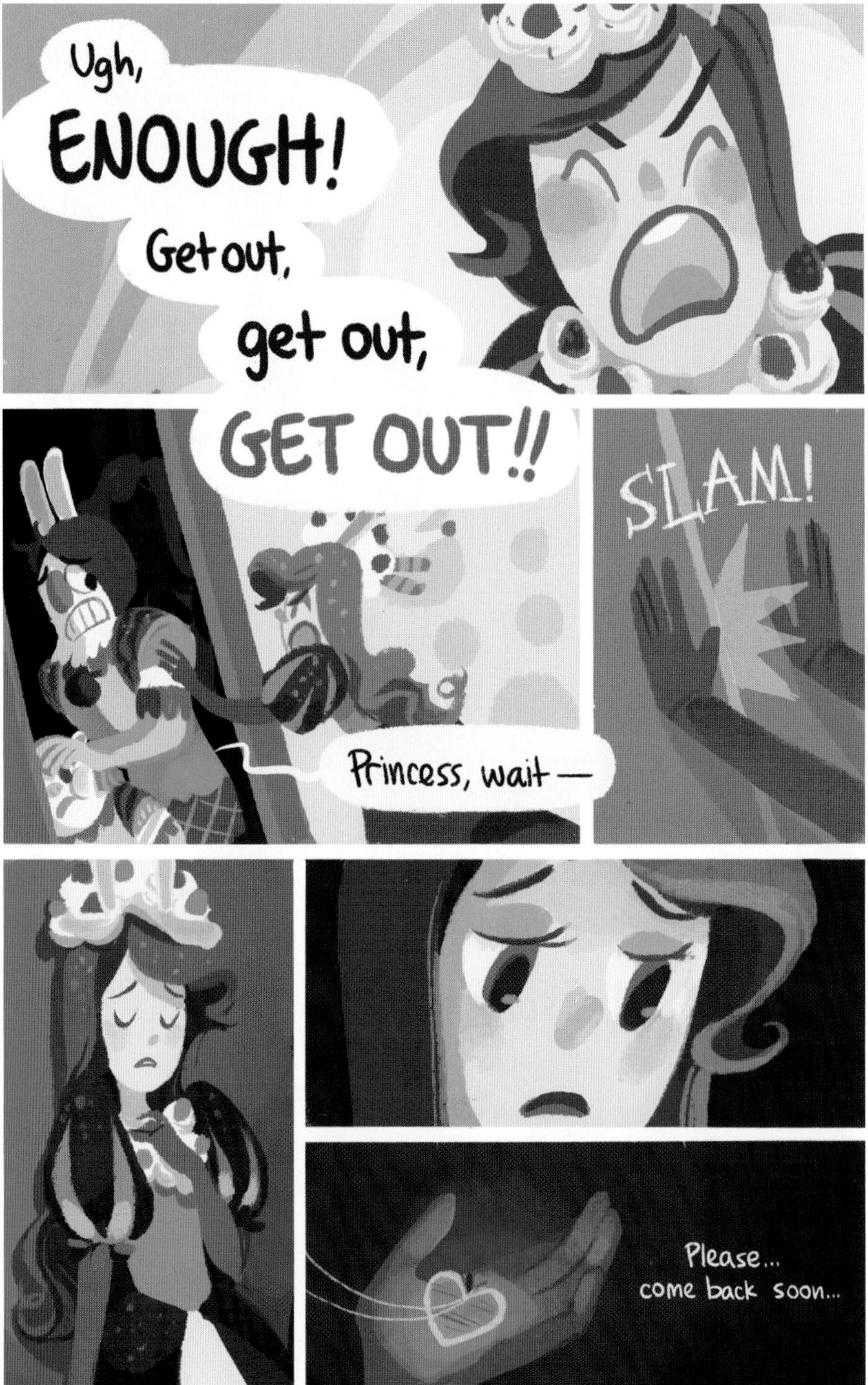
Ugh,
ENOUGH!
Get out,
get out,
GET OUT!!
SLAM!
Princess, wait—
Please... come back soon...

# Tiramisu Tower

Phew!
Is this it?

It's... kind of obvious for a thief's hideout.

Oh, we in the Royal Guard have known about this tower for ages.

You... have?

Why didn't you ever come raid the place, then?

Well, it's such a long **walk**... And it's so **hot**

Never mind.

Brambleby, is it?

Would you happen to be the butler?

Why would a thief have a...

squeak
squeak

Brambleby
(Butler)

W-Why does a thief have a butler?!

Well, I'm sure that taking care of all her stolen riches is quite the job.

I guess, but...

Forget all that!

We're here to see Saturday! Where the heck is she?

You've...

?

...got to be kidding me.

Gone fishin'
—Sat

Now what?

Pray tell us, Brambleby— where has Saturday gone, er... "fishin'"?

105

The Ripple Kingdom...

And I'm guessing she took the Dream Sword with her?

You're...

YES.

...really prepared, aren't you?

If she's gone to the Ripple Kingdom, we're in luck! There's a port not far from here.

Cool! Let's go!

Wait, though!

Shouldn't we stay and look around? You know, just so we don't miss anything?

Like **what**? We're just wasting time here.

But what if—

What if there's a huge treasure hoard upstairs?!

Come **on**, slowpokes!

Jeez!

huff huff huff huff

Yeah!

BOOT

GASP

SCORE!!

PFFT

Don't...tell me **all** of this was stolen from Caketown Castle.

Don't be ridiculous!

All of **that** was stolen from Caketown Castle!

hhhhhh

Hey, look!

It may not be the one we're looking for,

but it's still pretty nice!

You should try to find a new wand, Cuco!

And finally replace my old one...?

Oh no, don't get all sappy.

It's just— it's **hard**, okay?

That thing's special!

It's held together with tape.

well, yeahhhh

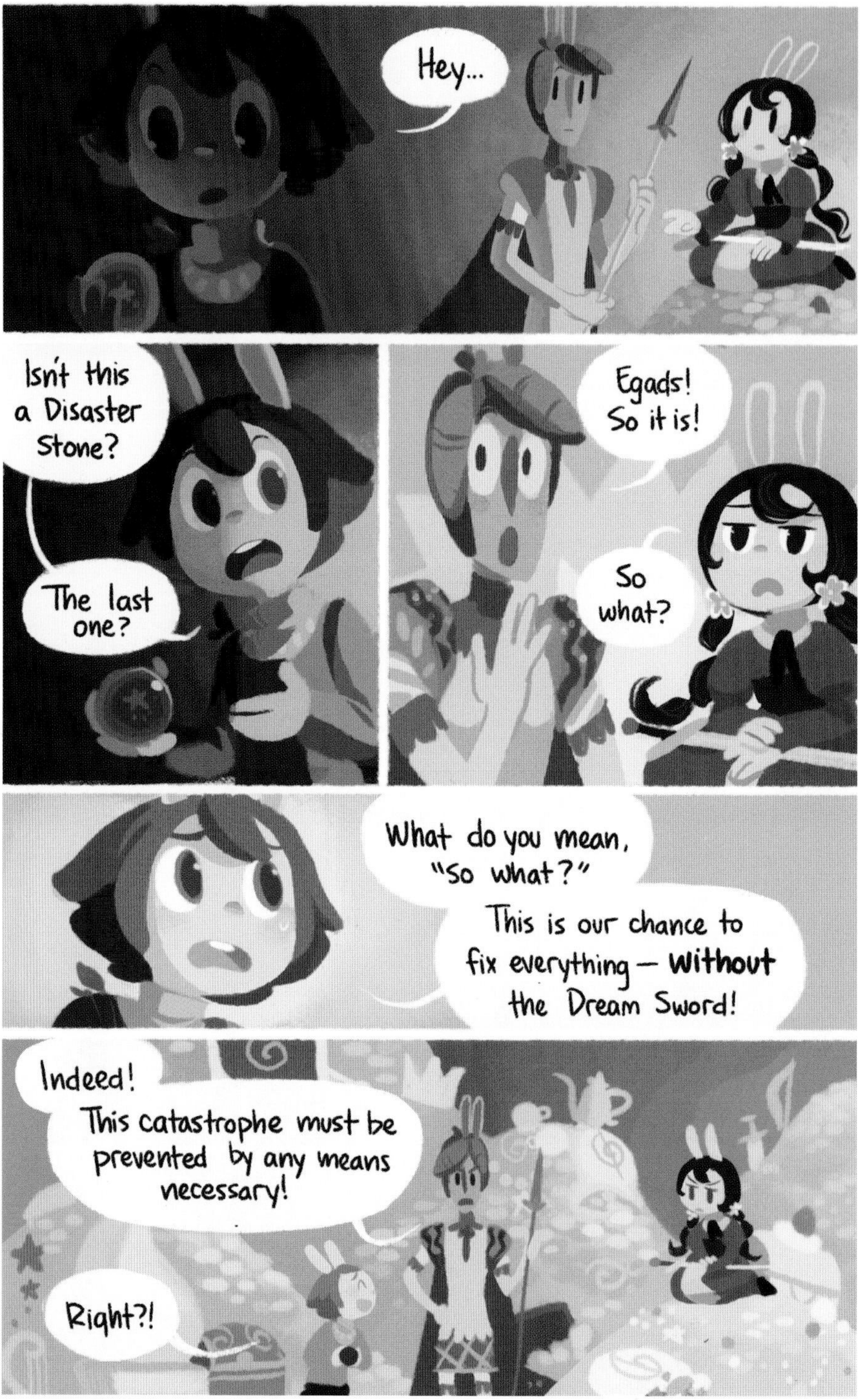
Hey...
Isn't this a Disaster Stone?
The last one?
Egads! So it is!
So what?
What do you mean, "So what?"
This is our chance to fix everything — **without** the Dream Sword!
Indeed!
This catastrophe must be prevented by any means necessary!
Right?!

But that's BORING!

You got me all worked up for this cool save-the-world adventure!

You can't just say "never mind, let's go home!"

You most certainly CAN!

Cucumber, we must take the stone!

No way! Let's find the sword!

uh

IRRESPONSIBLE BORING STUFFY
UNSAFE ~~ND~~ NO FUN LAME
WHO KNOWS ~~W~~ ~~TE~~ OF TI~
WHAT COULD HOW DUMB
~~HAPPEN TO~~

um

uh

Ooooh, are you guys fighting?

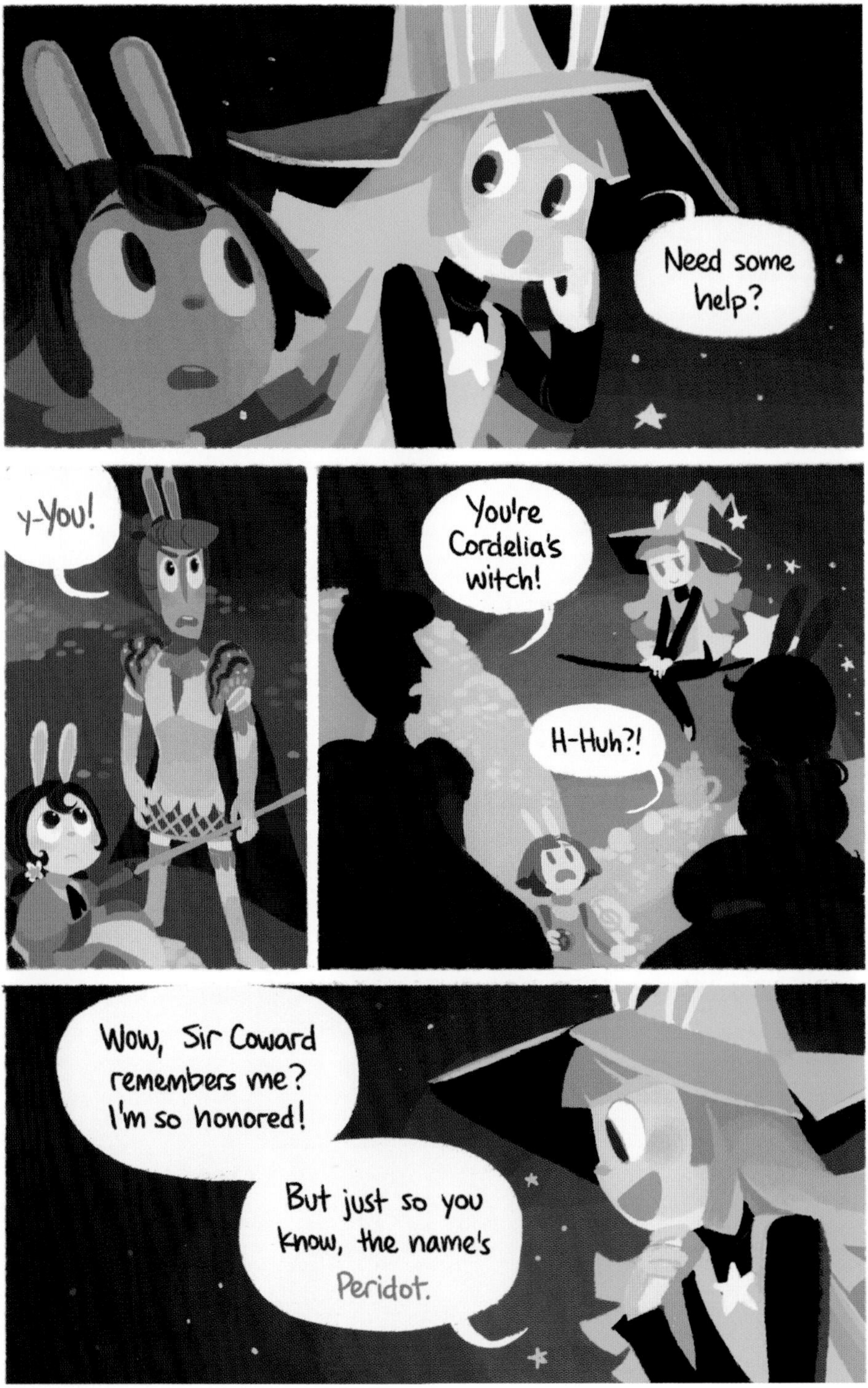

Need some help?
Y-You!
You're Cordelia's witch!
H-Huh?!
Wow, Sir Coward remembers me? I'm so honored!
But just so you know, the name's Peridot.

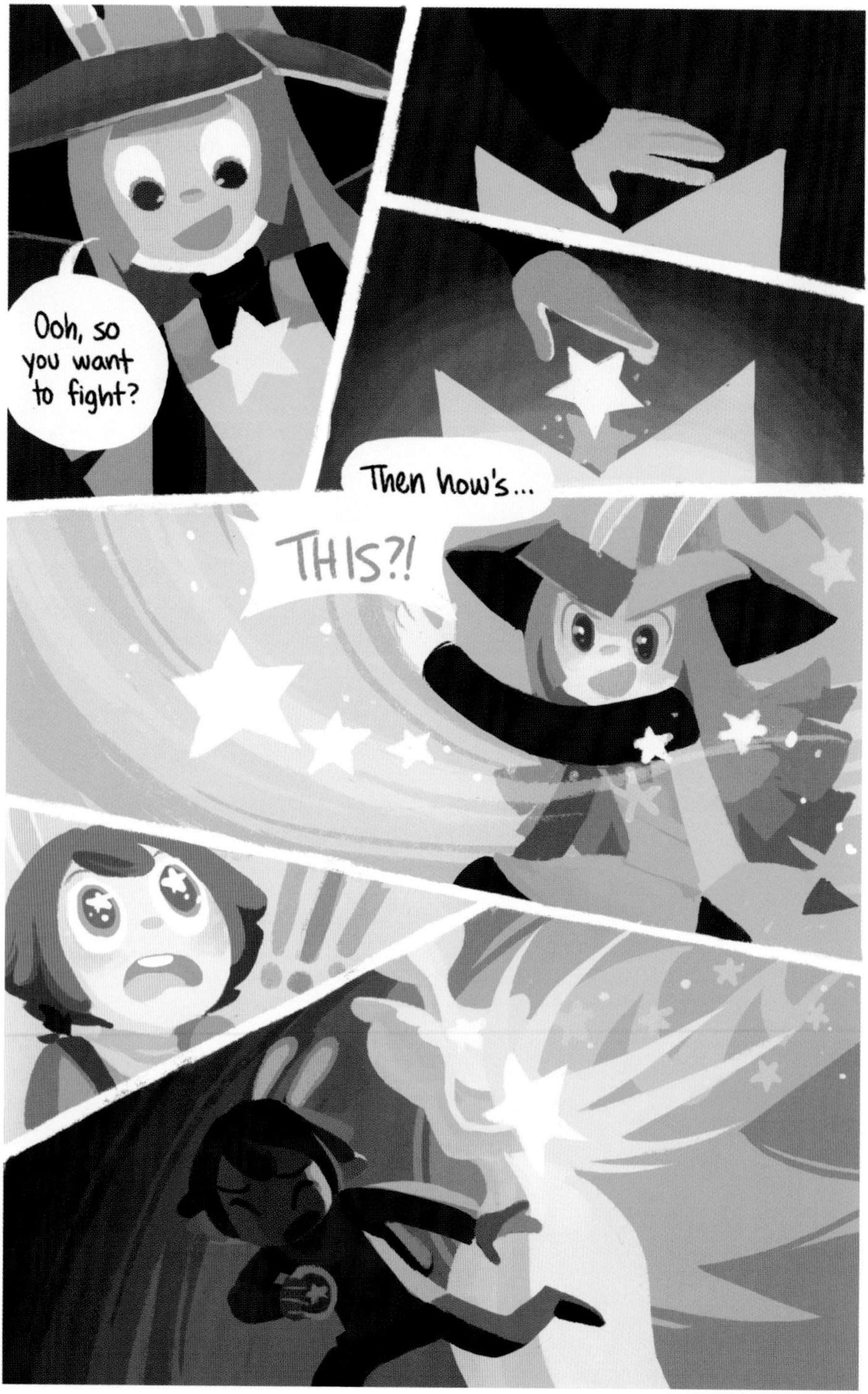
Ooh, so you want to fight?
Then how's...
THIS?!

W-Well, two can play at this game, Peridot!

Maybe it's about time I showed you my **OWN** specialt—

oh haha

**Now** are you feeling sappy?

Okay, Okay!!

H HA HA HA

Aww, poor baby!

Good thing you won't **need** a wand...

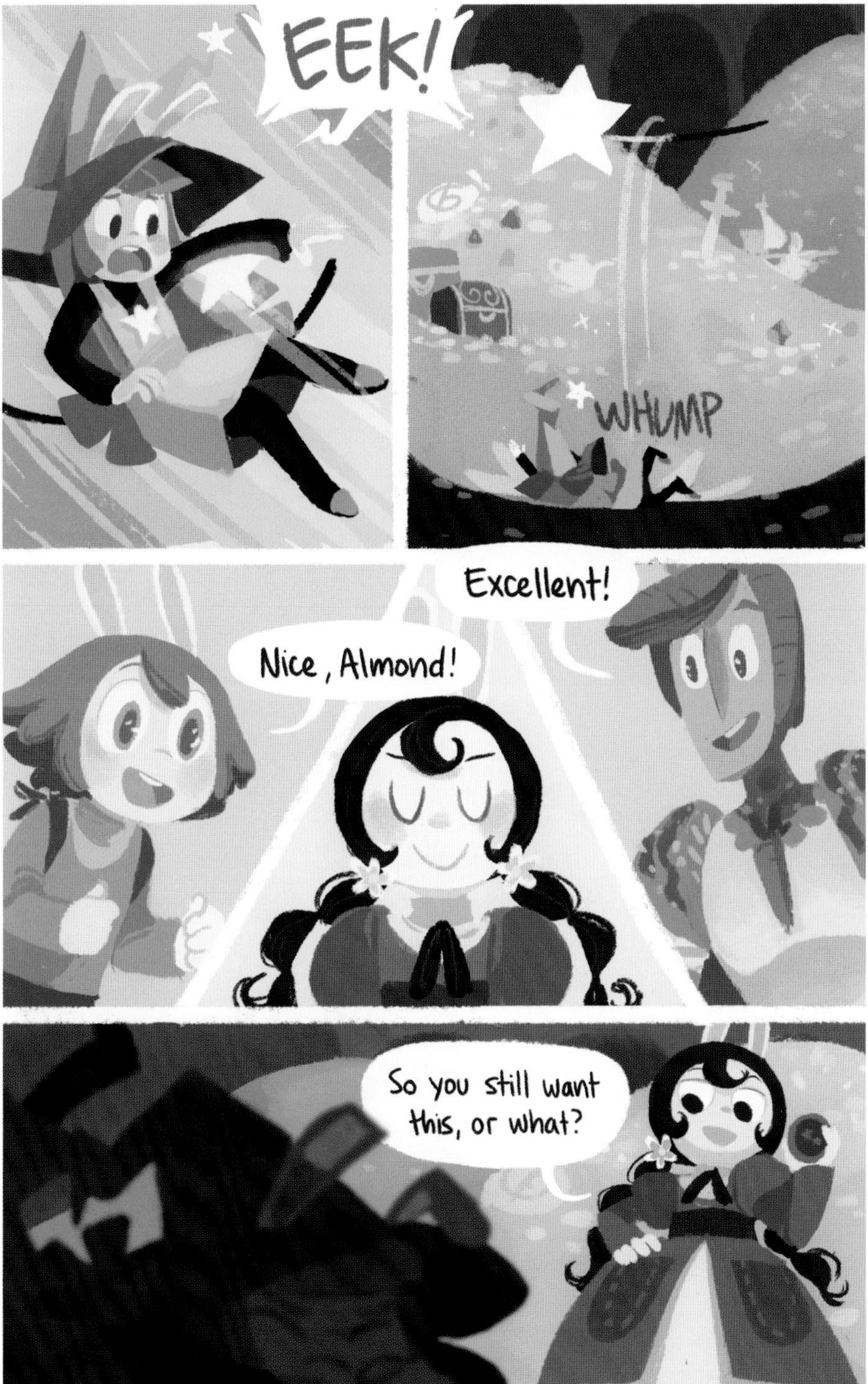
EEK!
WHUMP
Excellent!
Nice, Almond!
So you still want this, or what?

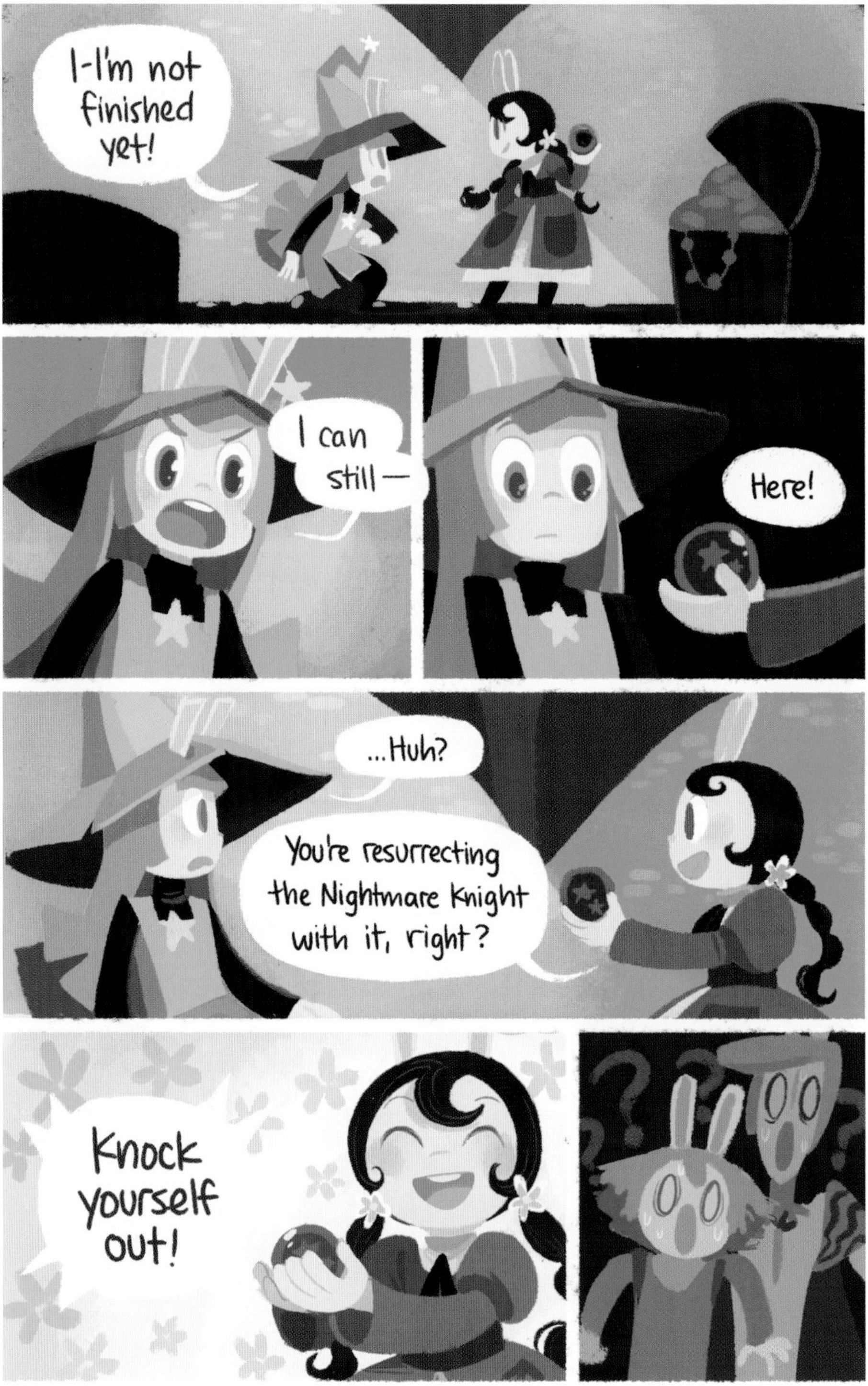

I-I'm not finished yet!
I can still—
Here!
...Huh?
You're resurrecting the Nightmare Knight with it, right?
Knock yourself out!

I...

I'm not taking this because I need your pity or anything, **Okay?!**

SWIPE

Sure, sure.

UGHHH!

Don't think this is over!

As soon as me and Cordelia have the Nightmare Knight on our side,

you're gonna **pay** for embarrassing me!!

NYAAAH!

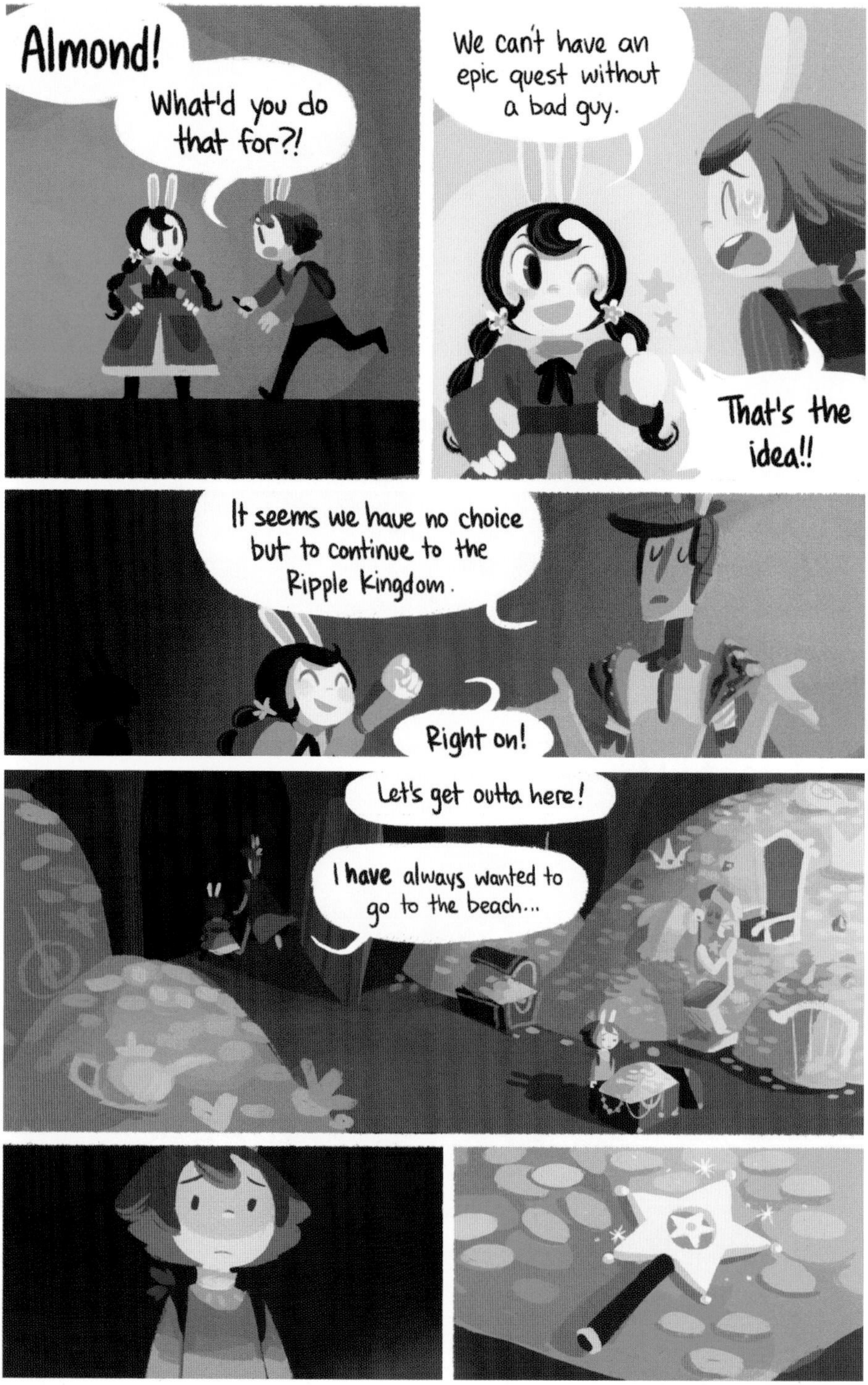
Almond!
What'd you do that for?!
We can't have an epic quest without a bad guy.
That's the idea!!
It seems we have no choice but to continue to the Ripple Kingdom.
Right on!
Let's get outta here!
I **have** always wanted to go to the beach...

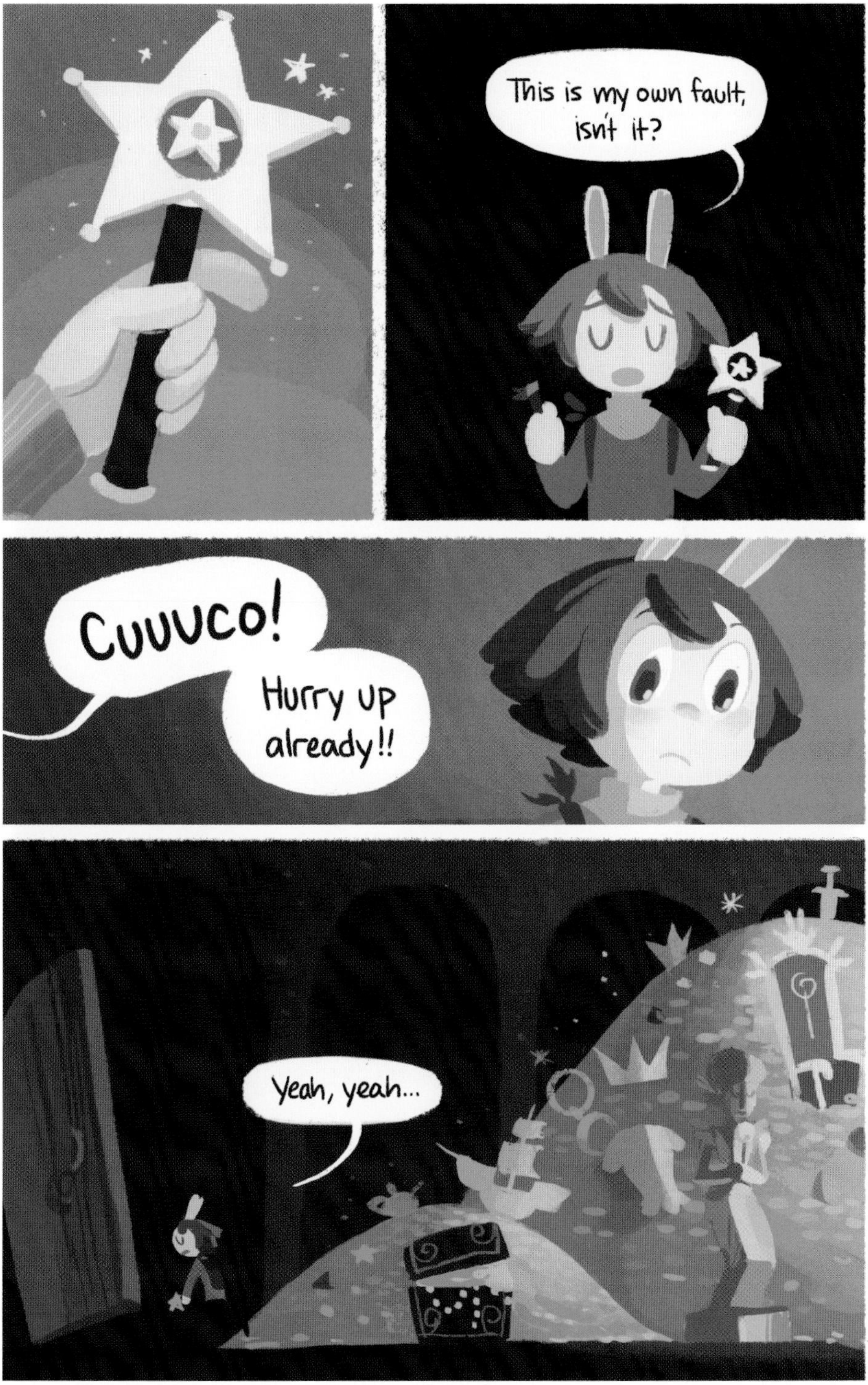
This is my own fault, isn't it?
Cuuuco!
Hurry up already!!
Yeah, yeah...

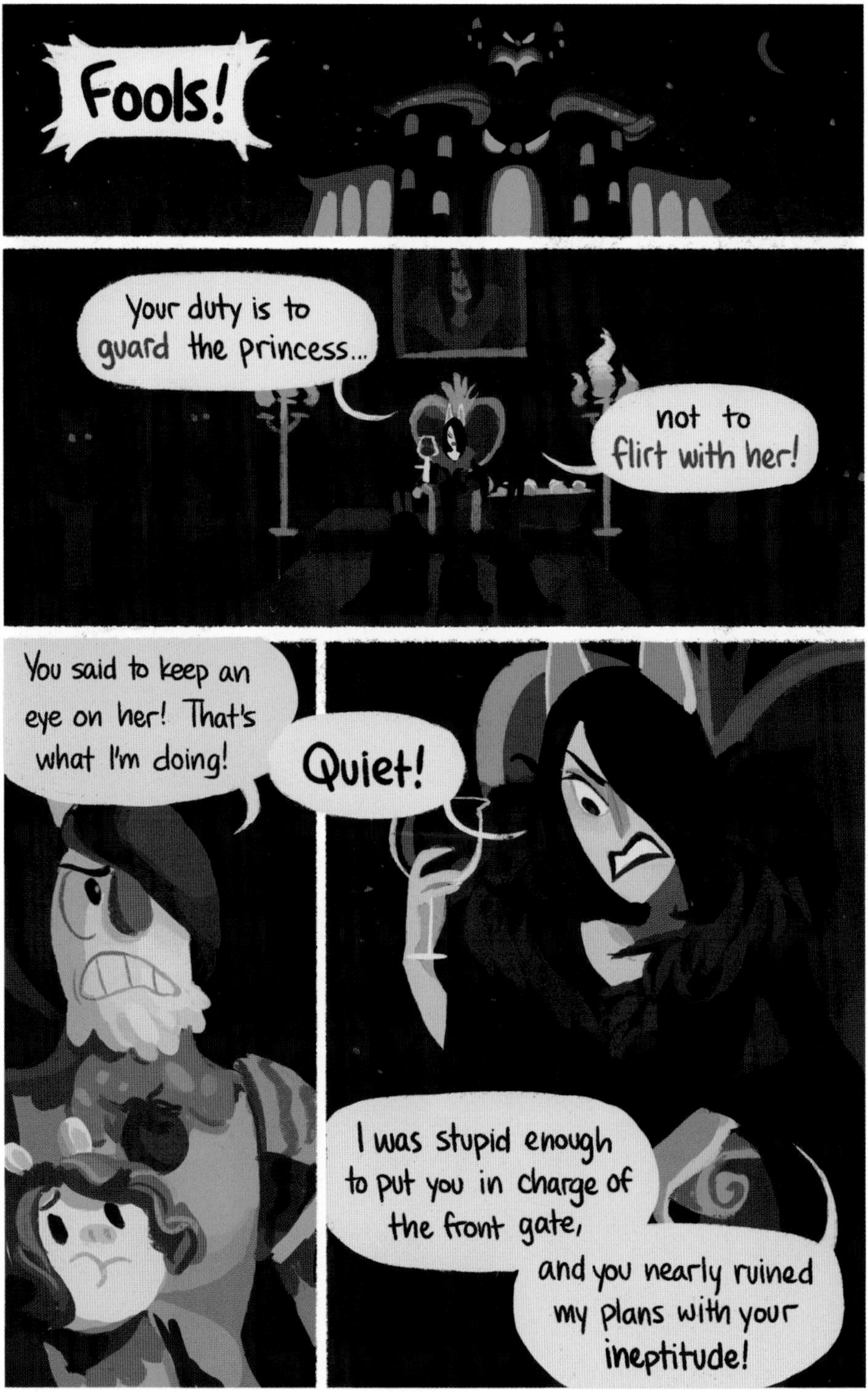
Fools!
Your duty is to guard the princess...
not to flirt with her!
You said to keep an eye on her! That's what I'm doing!
Quiet!
I was stupid enough to put you in charge of the front gate,
and you nearly ruined my plans with your ineptitude!

NOW GET OUT OF MY SIGHT!!

SLAM!!

I can't work with **anyone** on this planet.

creak

Oh, Your Maaajesty!

I'm hooooome!

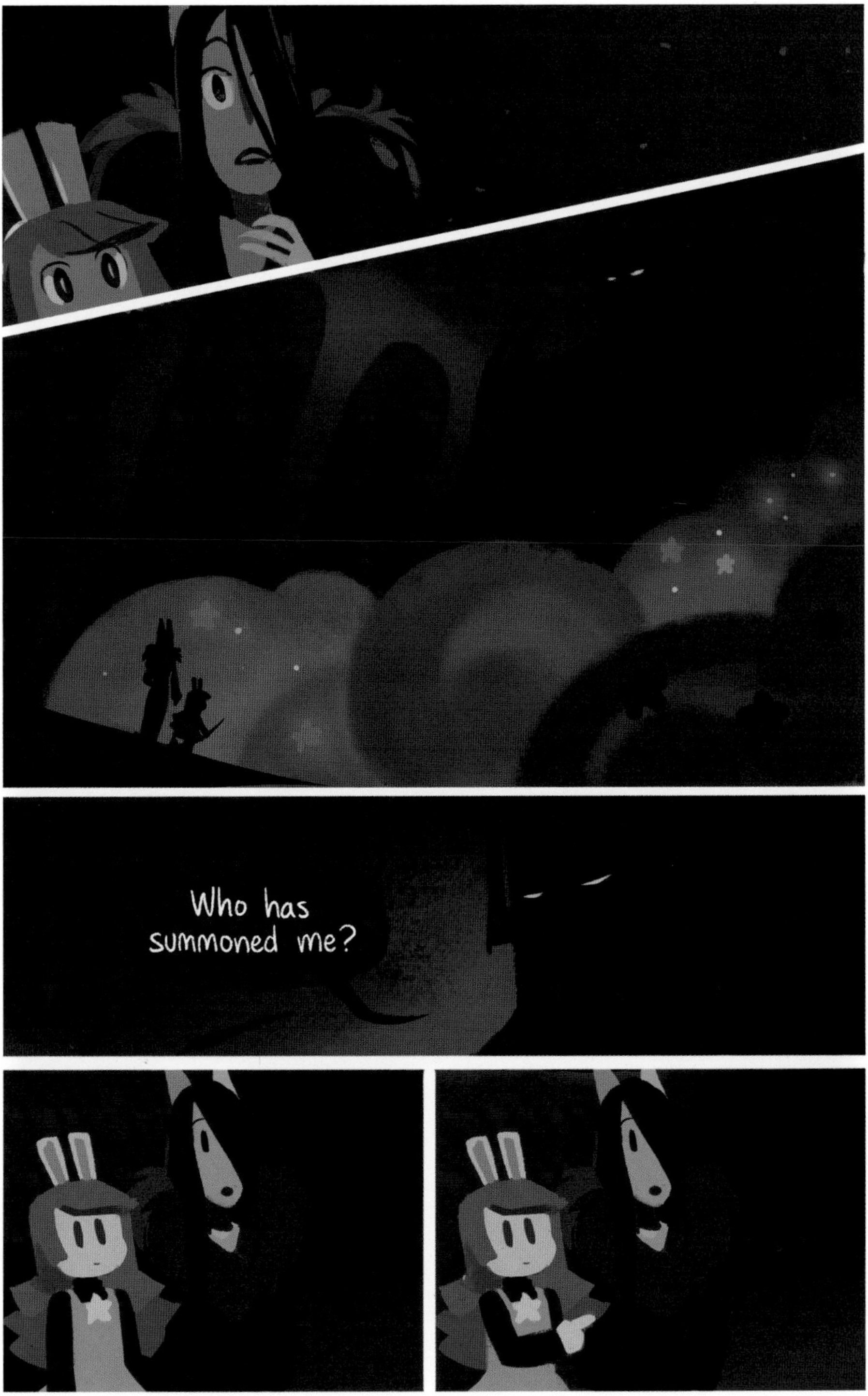
Who has
summoned me?

# Saltine

Thank you for choosing Breadboat Cruises!

Where can we take you today?

We wanna go to the Ripple Kingdom!

Nope!

Seastar Lagoon

SPACE

Oh! I'm sorry!

The truth is, we can't have anyone traveling there right now.

What ho! Is something amiss?

The other night, one of our ships was en route to the Ripple kingdom...

...when suddenly, it was under attack by...

a giant squid!!

How tough could a squid be, anyway?

I bet I could take him!

You can't just beat up everything, you know.

This is quite the predicament.

Surely there must be **some** way to cross the

sea

S-safely?

hee hee hee...

Hi.

Did you ladies and gentleman happen to say you were headed across the sea?

J-Just the one lady, actually—

Yeah, we did! Got a problem with that?

No, no!

Quite the opposite, actually.

Hee, hee.

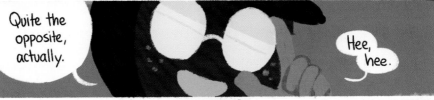

Allow me to introduce myself. I'm Cosmo, an up-and-coming inventor.

Well, I'm Almond, an up-and-coming legendary hero!

These are my sidekicks, Cucumber and Carrot.

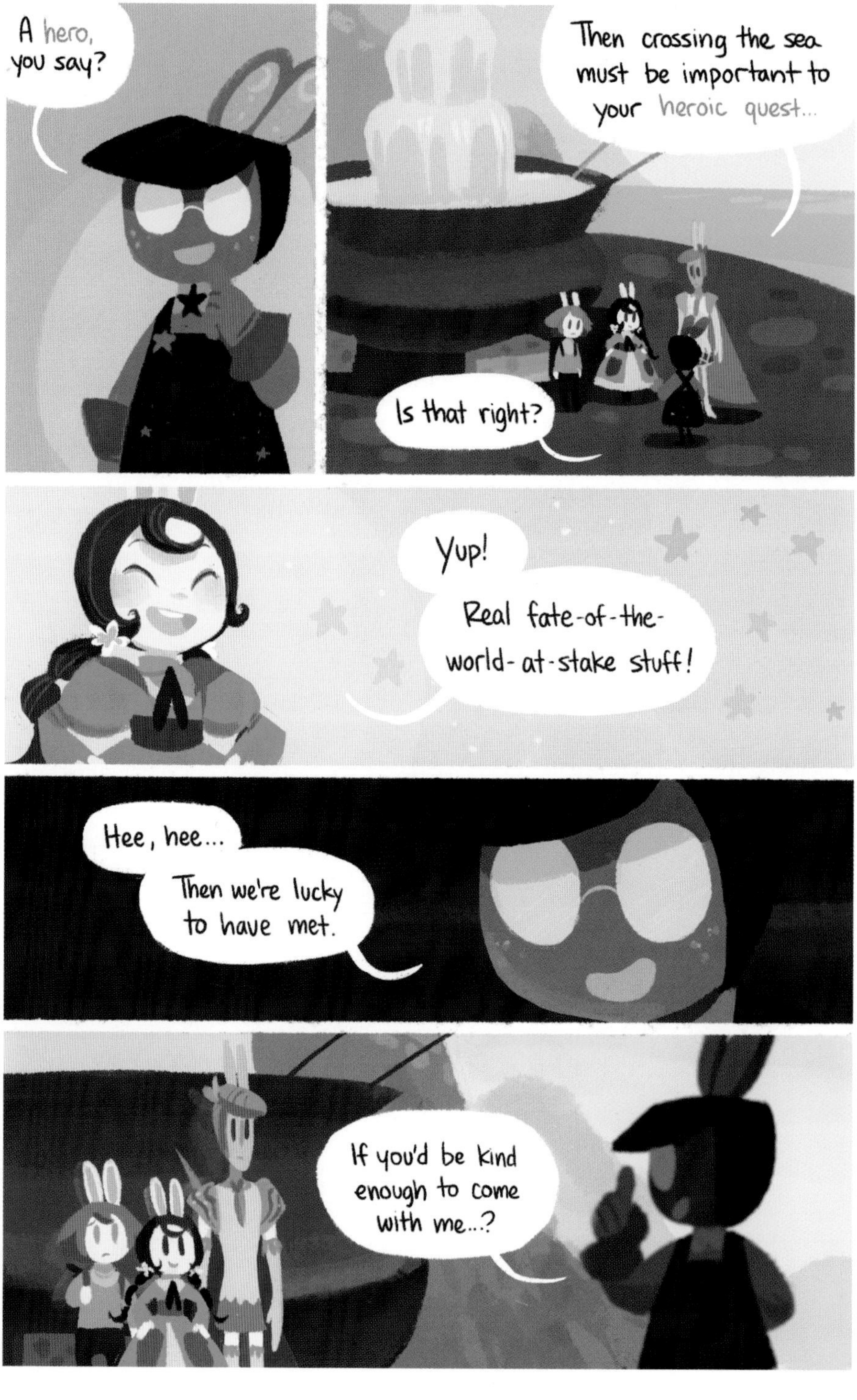
A hero, you say?
Then crossing the sea must be important to your heroic quest...
Is that right?
Yup!
Real fate-of-the-world-at-stake stuff!
Hee, hee...
Then we're lucky to have met.
If you'd be kind enough to come with me...?

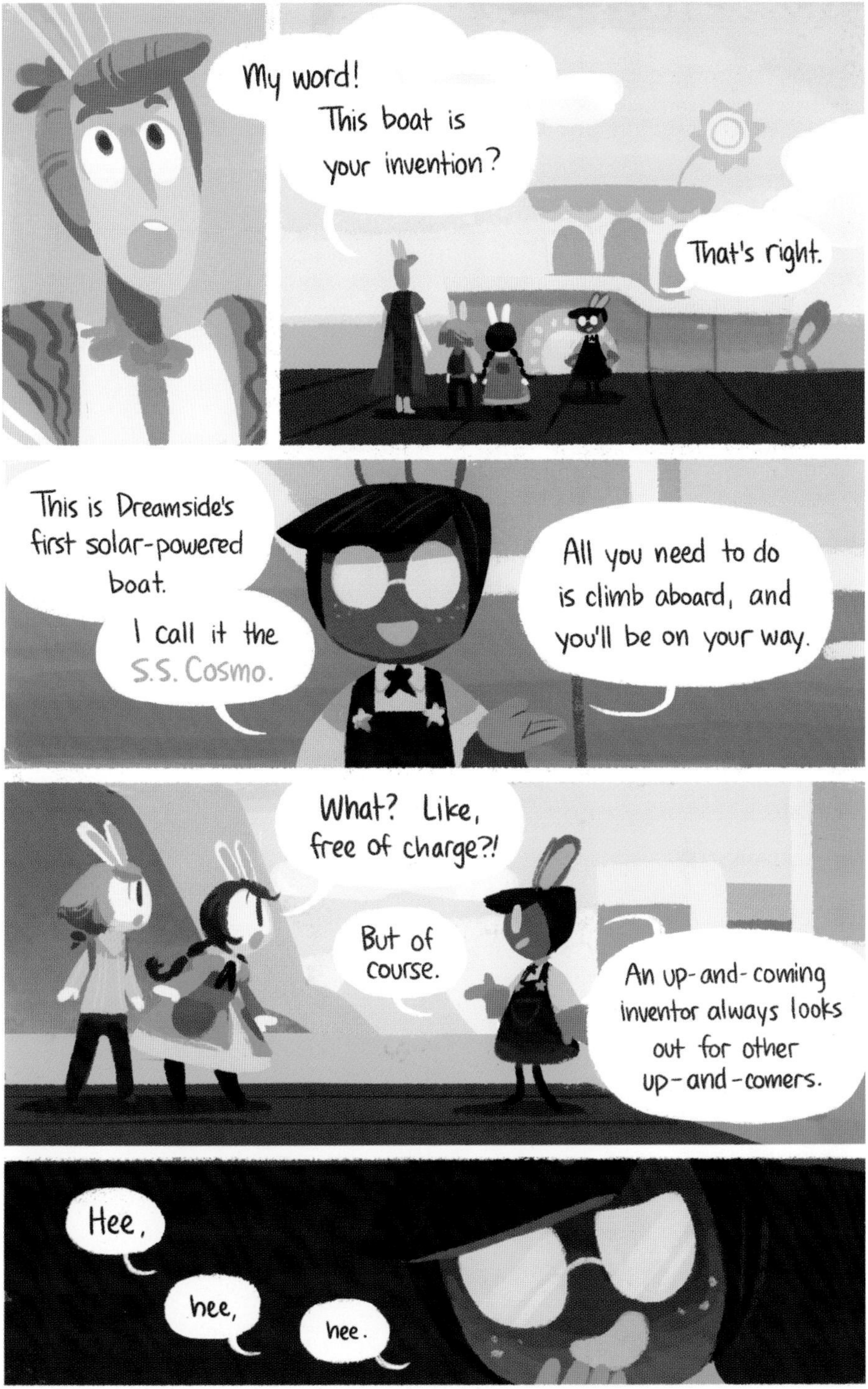
My word!
This boat is your invention?
That's right.
This is Dreamside's first solar-powered boat.
I call it the S.S. Cosmo.
All you need to do is climb aboard, and you'll be on your way.
What? Like, free of charge?!
But of course.
An up-and-coming inventor always looks out for other up-and-comers.
Hee,
hee,
hee.

I

don't like this.

Come **on**, Cuco! What other options do we have?

But this is weird!

Tell me this isn't weird!

Ahem.

Cucumber, if I may?

I understand your feelings completely...

but if we refuse this strange child's offer, we'll be stranded here indefinitely.

I know I'm going to regret this, though...

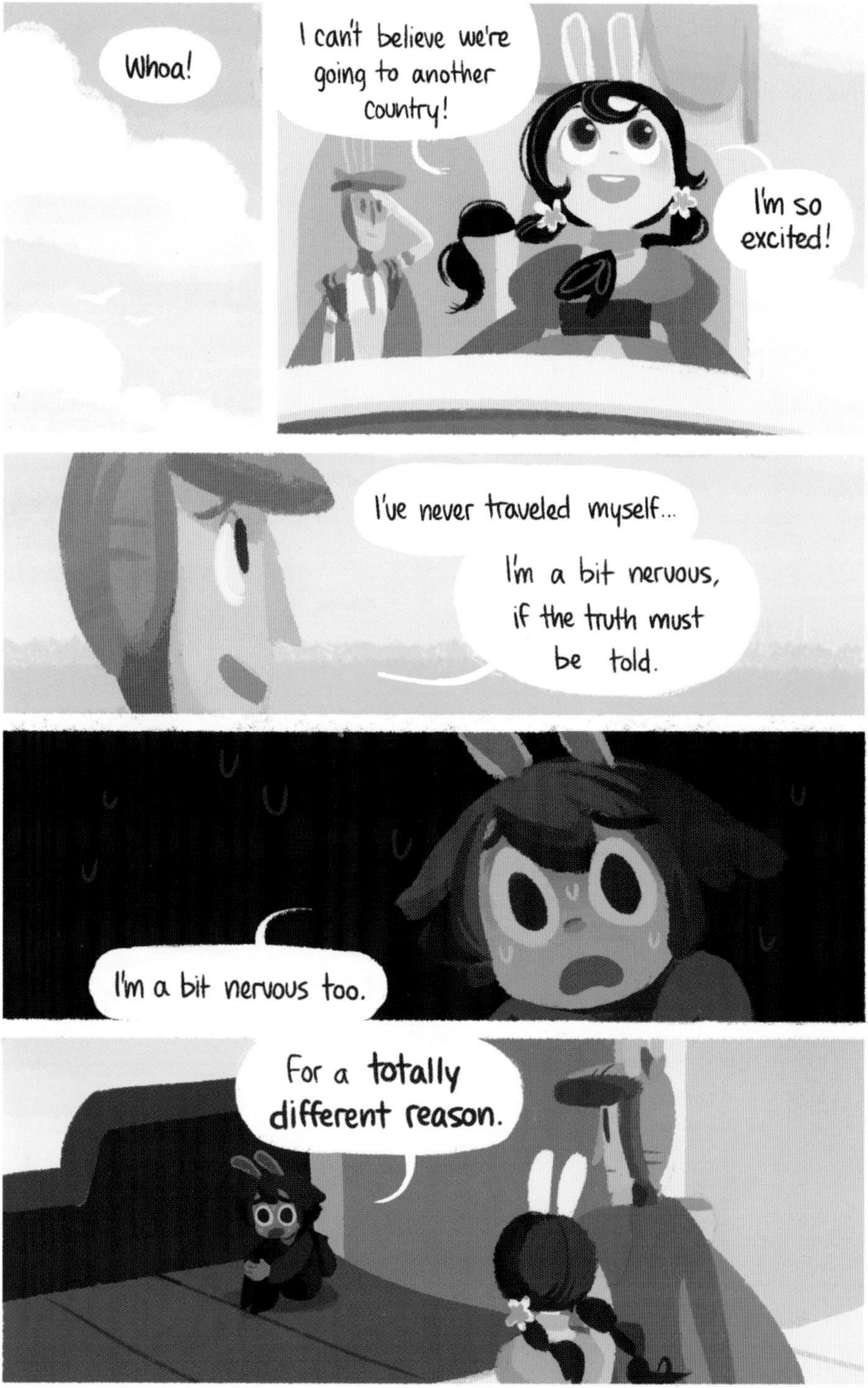
Whoa!
I can't believe we're going to another country!
I'm so excited!
I've never traveled myself...
I'm a bit nervous, if the truth must be told.
I'm a bit nervous too.
For a totally different reason.

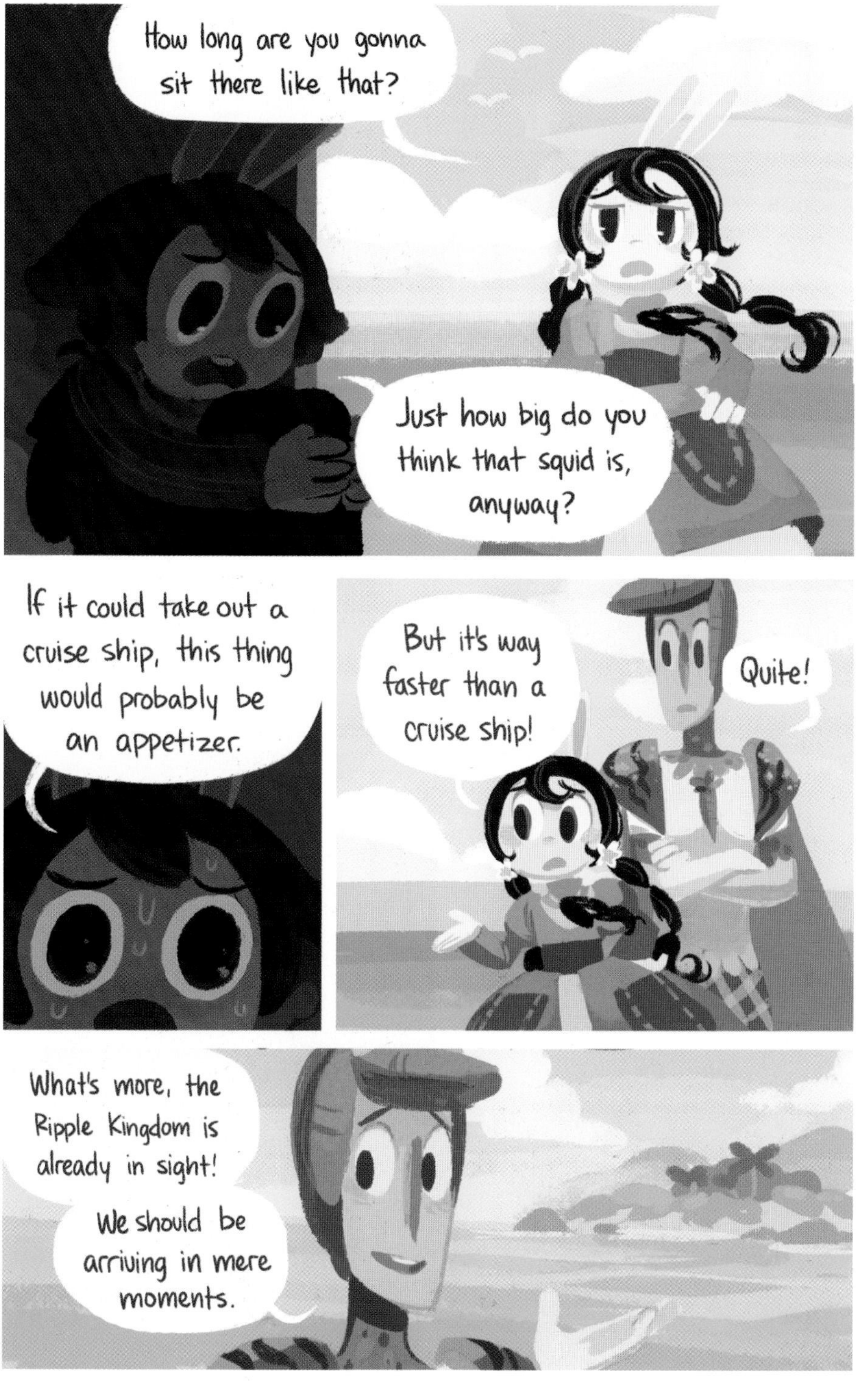
How long are you gonna sit there like that?
Just how big do you think that squid is, anyway?
If it could take out a cruise ship, this thing would probably be an appetizer.
But it's way faster than a cruise ship!
Quite!
What's more, the Ripple Kingdom is already in sight!
We should be arriving in mere moments.

M-Maybe you're right.

I guess I am worrying a little too much, huh?

Uh, **yeah!**

And, you know, maybe this isn't so bad.

Being on the open ocean, heading for a new country...

...with the wind in my hair, and the sun shining **oh my gosh where did the sun go**

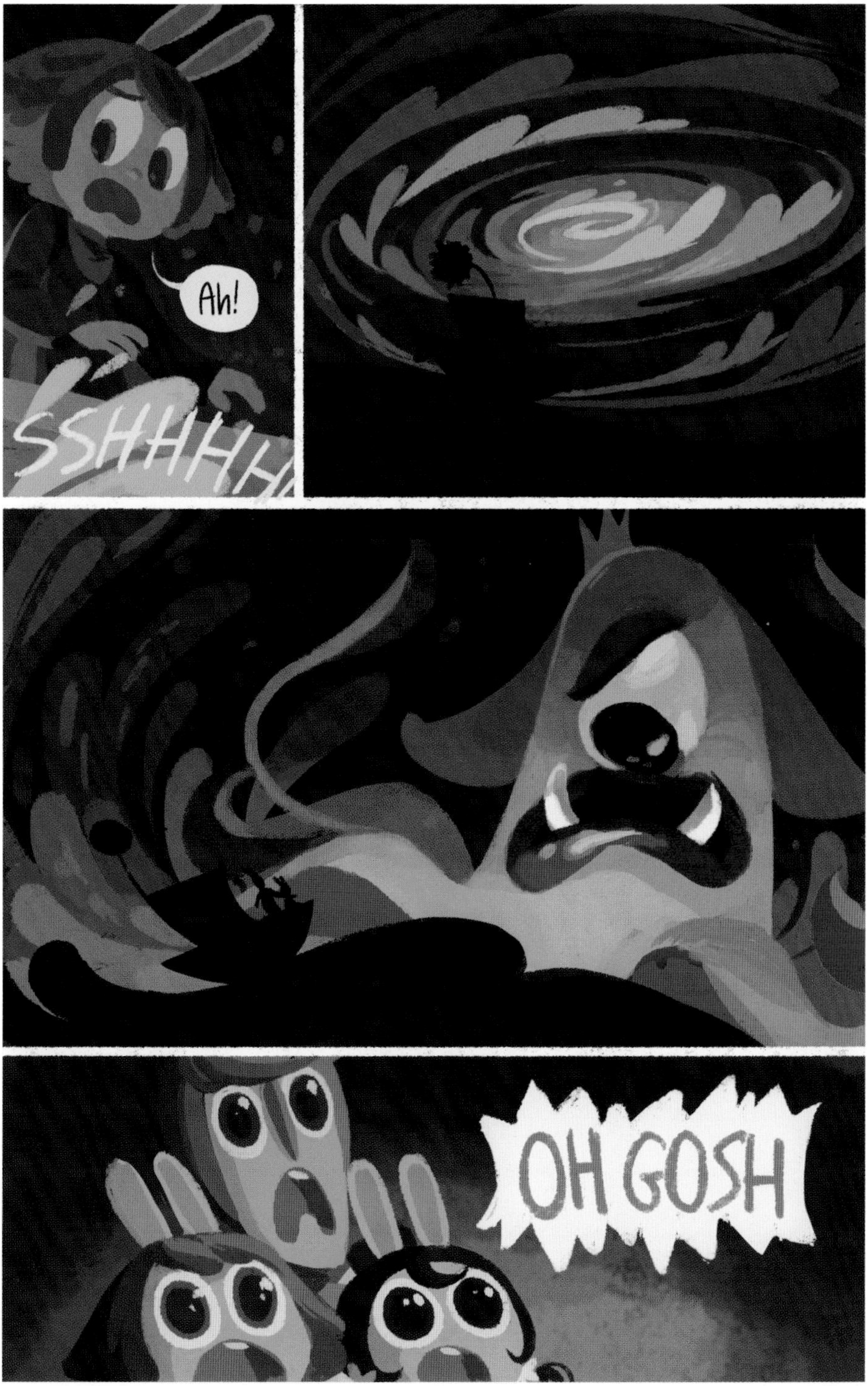
Ah!
SSHHHHH
OH GOSH

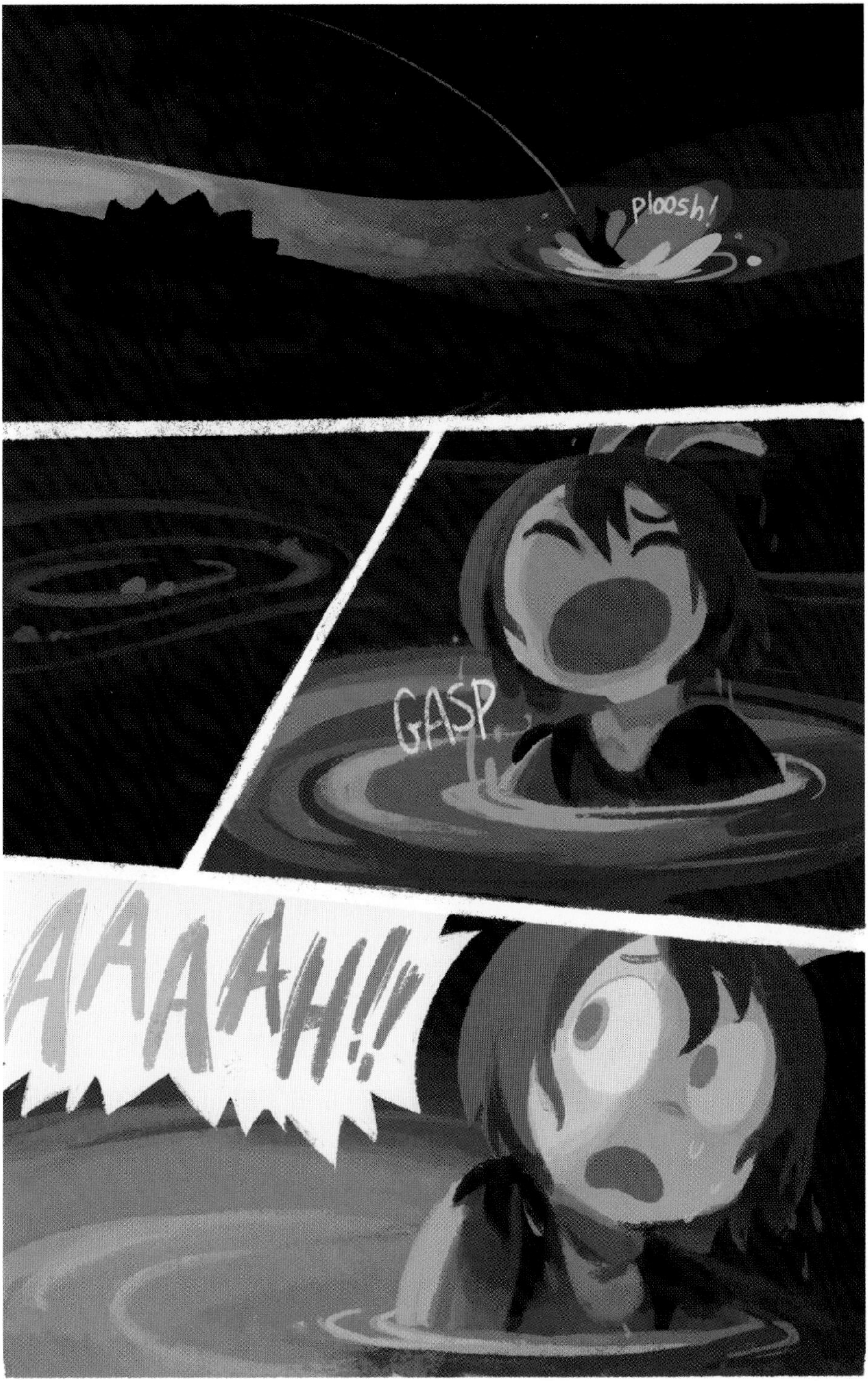
Ploosh!
GASP
AAAAH!!

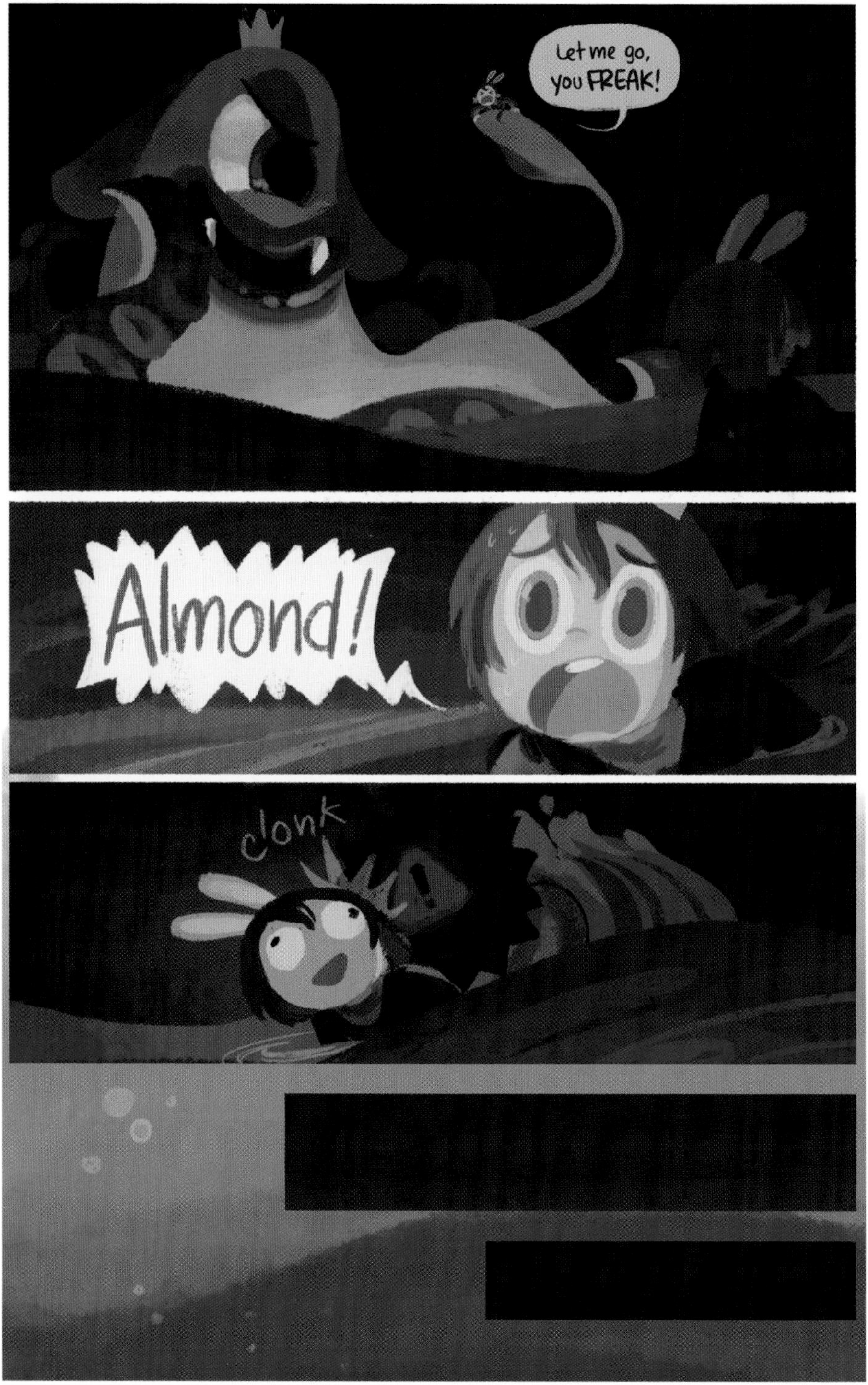
Let me go, you FREAK!
Almond!
clonk
[redacted]
[redacted]

To be continued in...

Cucumber QUEST 2

The Ripple Kingdom

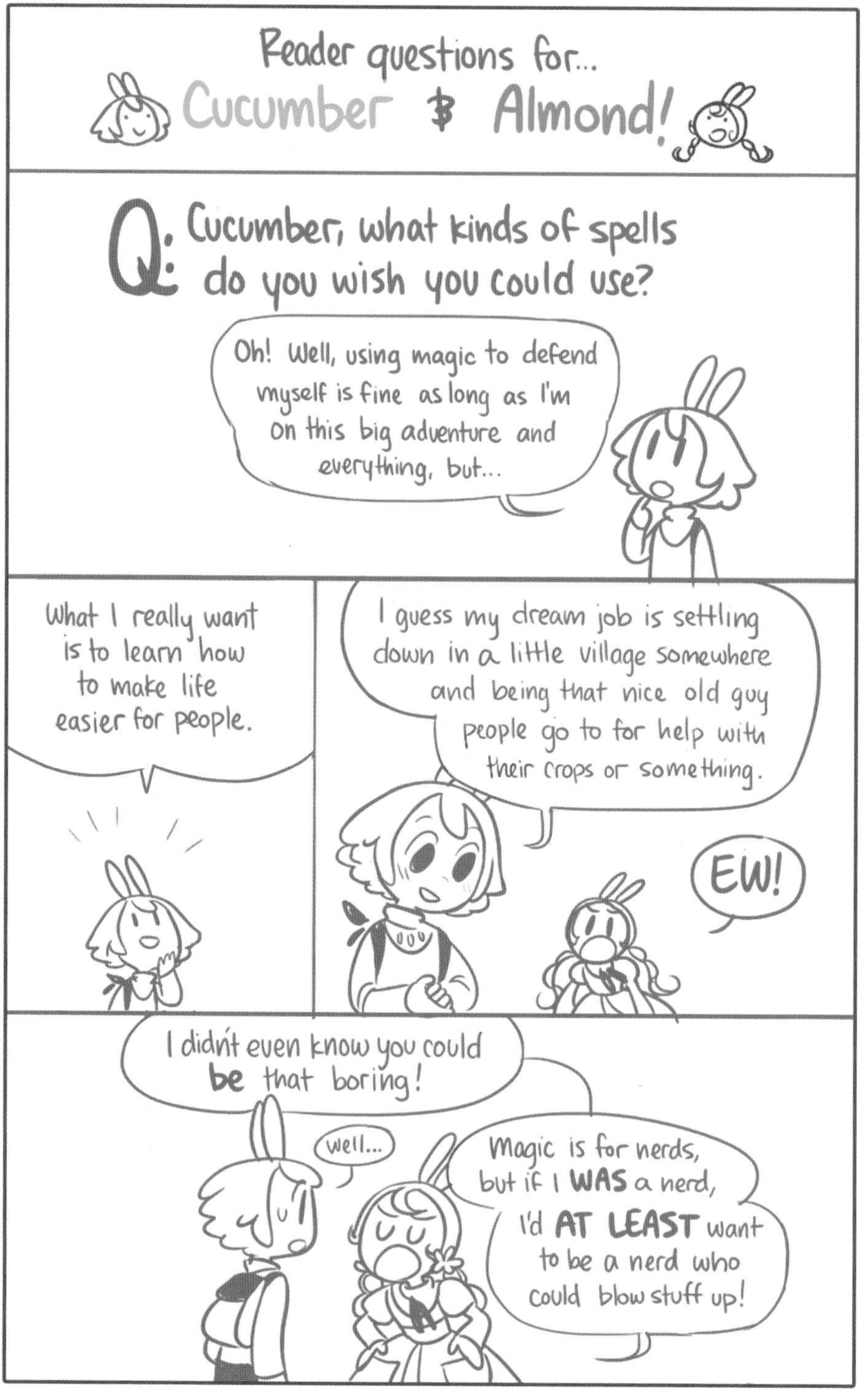
Reader questions for...
Cucumber & Almond!
Q: Cucumber, what kinds of spells do you wish you could use?
Oh! Well, using magic to defend myself is fine as long as I'm on this big adventure and everything, but...
What I really want is to learn how to make life easier for people.
I guess my dream job is settling down in a little village somewhere and being that nice old guy people go to for help with their crops or something.
EW!
I didn't even know you could **be** that boring!
well...
Magic is for nerds, but if I **WAS** a nerd, I'd **AT LEAST** want to be a nerd who could blow stuff up!

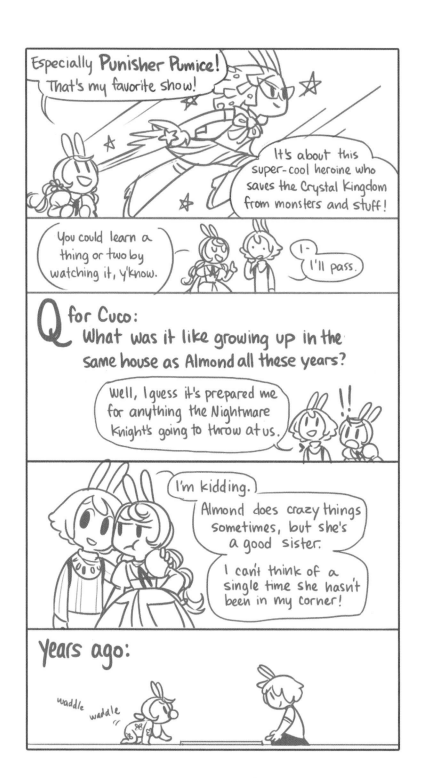

Especially **Punisher Pumice!** That's my favorite show!

It's about this super-cool heroine who saves the Crystal Kingdom from monsters and stuff!

You could learn a thing or two by watching it, y'know.

I- I'll pass.

**Q** for Cuco: What was it like growing up in the same house as Almond all these years?

Well, I guess it's prepared me for anything the Nightmare Knight's going to throw at us.

!!

I'm kidding.

Almond does crazy things sometimes, but she's a good sister.

I can't think of a single time she hasn't been in my corner!

years ago:

waddle waddle

# Reader questions for...
# Cabbage $ Bagel!

**Q:** Cabbage, what do you do all day to pass the time in that prison cell?

Listen, kids at home— reading is fuel for the imagination!

Reading! What the heck else is there to do in this dump?!

When I open a book, I feel like I have the freedom to just walk out of this cell whenever I want.

You **DO** have the

Like this one!

One of my favorites in college, and still a favorite now!

Really changed my outlook on life, let me tell ya.

The Importance of Being Paid
oscar mayer

**Q:** Cabbage, when was the first time Cucumber failed you miserably?

Oh, I remember that one.

Reader questions for: Bacon & Tomato!

Q: Bacon, what kinds of video games do you play?

Oh, uhhh

shooters.

actually

Chiffon
Welcome home, master!

Q: Bacon, tell me about your dreams and aspirations!

Huh?

Well, last night, I dreamed I was rolling around on a giant pizza.

It was awful, though, 'cause it had bell peppers on it and I hate those.

And I'm not sure what you mean by the second thing, but I do sweat a lot during the summer—

Aspirations, you clown!

Look, I don't know what kind of answer you're expecting to get out of this guy, but just **look** at him!

Not exactly reach-for-the-stars material!

You're so mean, sir...

If you ask me, he **should** be dreaming about becoming a fraction as manly as I am!

Not that it's possible, of course.

Q: Tomato, what do you do to your hair every day to keep it so perfect?

Hair care is a necessity for any manly man.

I know what you're thinking, my loyal fans, and let me tell you something.

Luckily for me, my luscious locks look this good naturally. Don't even have to touch 'em!

Like, I do his hair every morning.

sh-**SHH!**

Doesn't anybody know how to keep a secret around here?!

# Sir Carrot

Atk ★★★
Def ★★★★
Sp ★★

⚔ flimsy spear
💗 strawberry pendant
ᗐ folded napkin

This honorable knight from Caketown has dedicated his life to protecting his king, Croissant, and his true love, Princess Parfait. He **did** run away while their castle was being attacked, but his heart is in the right place, and he's doing what he can to save them. Let's just hope they're patient.

# Princess Parfait

Atk ★
Def ★
Bon ★★★★

✉ heartfelt letter
💗 carrot pendant
📕 picture book

Parfait, the Doughnut Kingdom's beloved princess, faithfully awaits the return of her knight in candy-coated armor...but life in captivity is getting a little hard to bear. If only she had someone looking out for her...

# Cosmo

What is this kid's **DEAL?!**

# Peridot

| | | | |
|---|---|---|---|
| Atk | better than Almond | ★ | wand-broom |
| Def | better than Almond | 🧹 | witch's hat |
| Sp | better than Almond | 📖 | comic book |

Professional minion, unparalleled magical prodigy, cutest girl in Dreamside... Yep, Peridot's pretty much the best, and she wants **everyone** to know it. But can you blame her? (Uh–don't answer that, or she'll turn you to stone.)

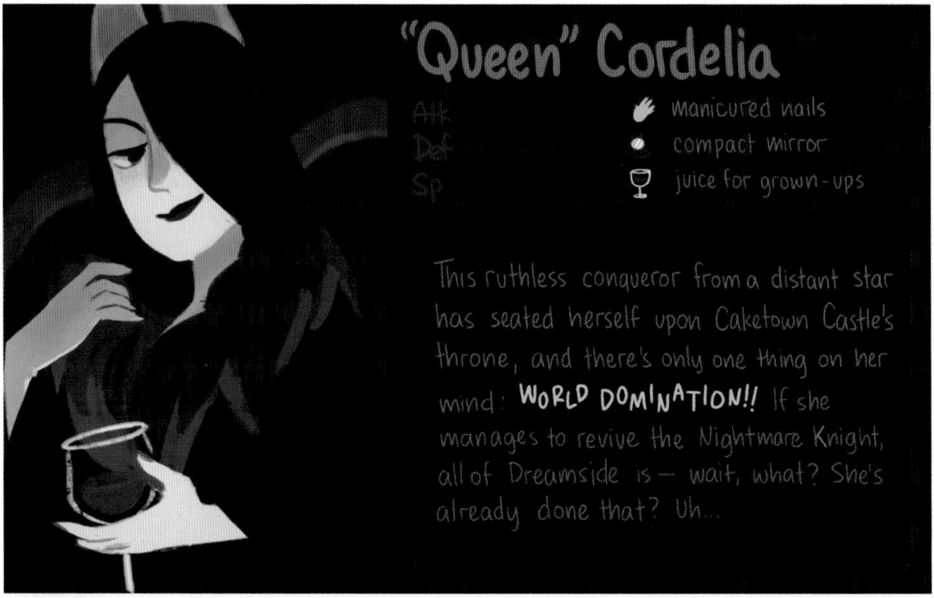
"Queen" Cordelia
Atk
Def
Sp
manicured nails
compact mirror
juice for grown-ups
This ruthless conqueror from a distant star has seated herself upon Caketown Castle's throne, and there's only one thing on her mind: WORLD DOMINATION!! If she manages to revive the Nightmare Knight, all of Dreamside is — wait, what? She's already done that? Uh...

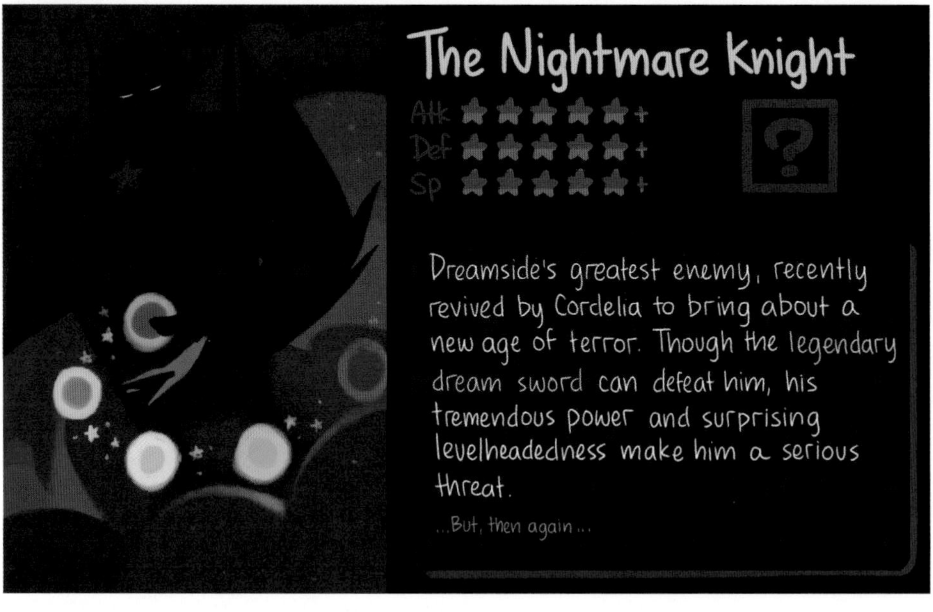
The Nightmare Knight
Atk +
Def +
Sp +
?
Dreamside's greatest enemy, recently revived by Cordelia to bring about a new age of terror. Though the legendary dream sword can defeat him, his tremendous power and surprising levelheadedness make him a serious threat.
...But, then again...

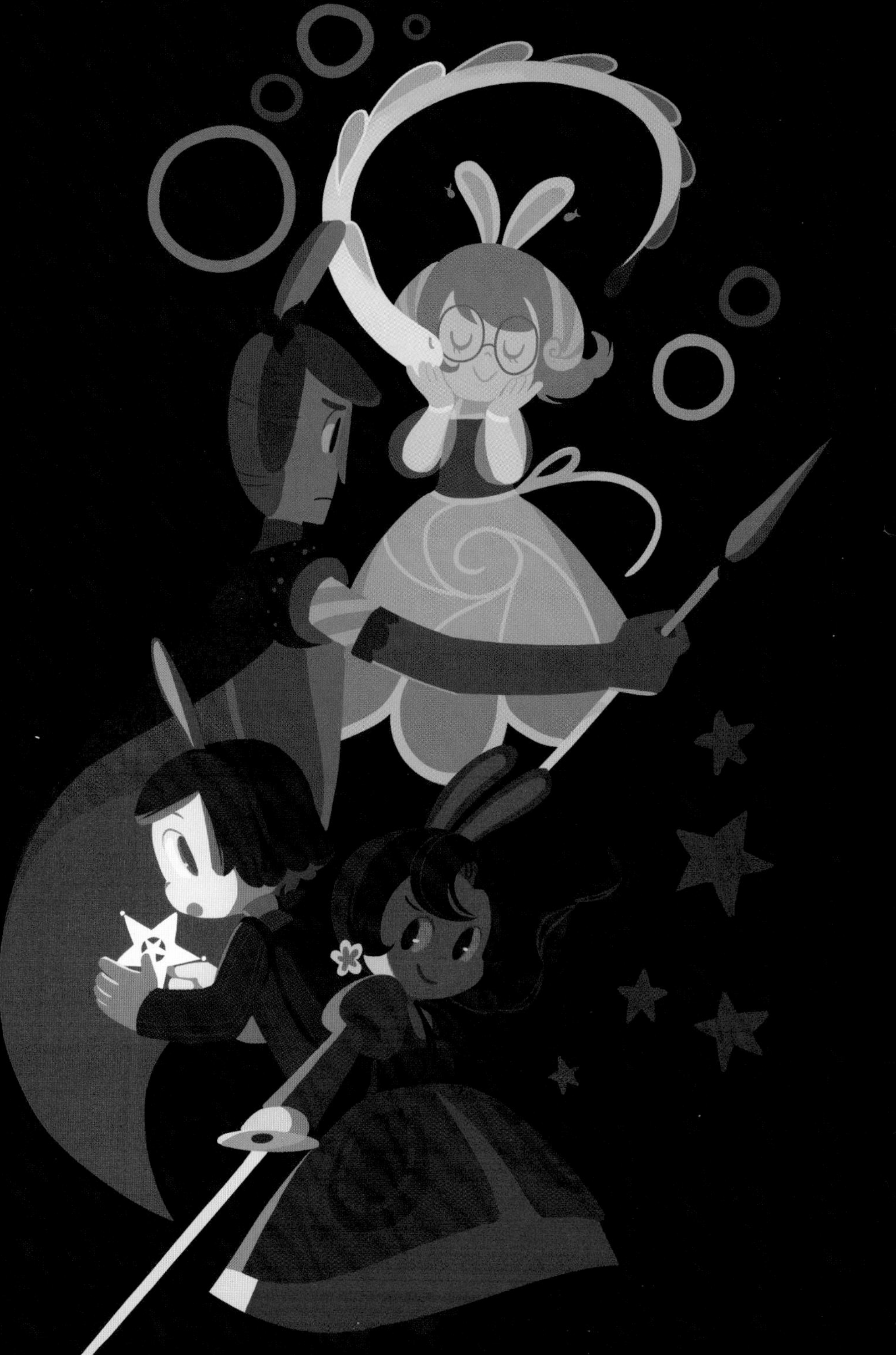

# welcome to
# Dreamside!

Floating somewhere among the stars is a flat
little world where dreams come true. Where
did it come from? What awaits in its future?
Why is its sun a giant smiley face?

None of those questions will be answered in this
section. But we *can* take a brief tour, at least.
Let's go!

# The Doughnut Kingdom

The culinary (and literal) center of the world, home to gumdrop trees, sugary mountains, and our heroes, Cucumber and Almond. We've left this kingdom behind for now, but there's more we haven't seen.

Folks from this kingdom have rounded bunny ears.

# The Ripple Kingdom

Ocean lovers love this place! The pristine beaches and coral forests make it the perfect vacation spot. Just make sure you've got a reservation if you're headed for the very exclusive Crabster Resort.

Folks from this kingdom have ears that bend out slightly.

# The Melody Kingdom

The people of Trebleopolis really know how to throw a party, and Queen Cymbal's birthday is right around the corner. But stay alert! Rumor has it that *ghosts* haunt the northern end of the island. Good thing Intermezzo Wall keeps them out...

Folks from this kingdom have ears that fold over.

## The Flower Kingdom

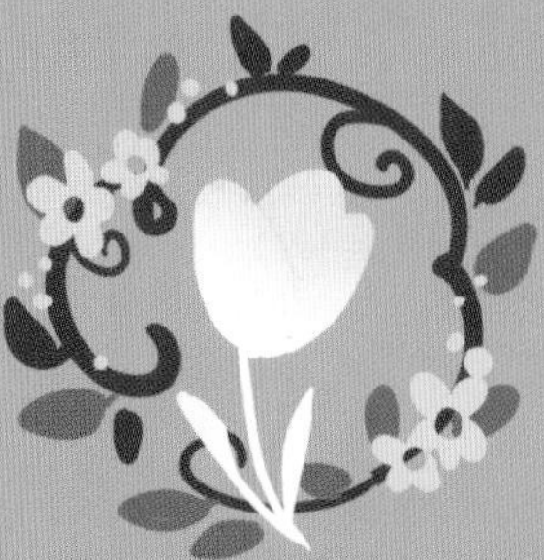

Style lovers and explorers, come on down! Botanica Springs, home of the world-famous *R* fashion magazine, is built atop the ruins of an ancient civilization. Who knows what treasures could be growing there?

Folks from this kingdom have ears that sprout at the ends.

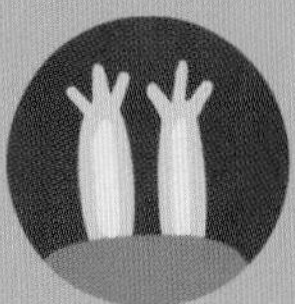

## The Crystal Kingdom

A land of opposites, made up of two regions with rulers of their own. Westward, a scary secret sleeps in the frozen wilderness outside Quartzton. Eastward, a hot spot in Basaltbury welcomes those who feel lucky. In the center of it all is the home of *Punisher Pumice*, Almond's favorite TV show.

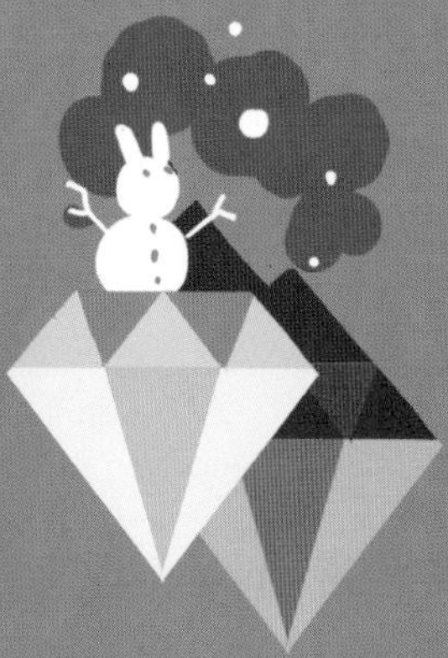

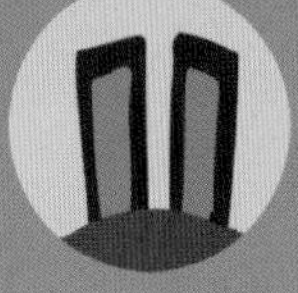

Folks from this kingdom have rectangular ears.

## The Sky Kingdom

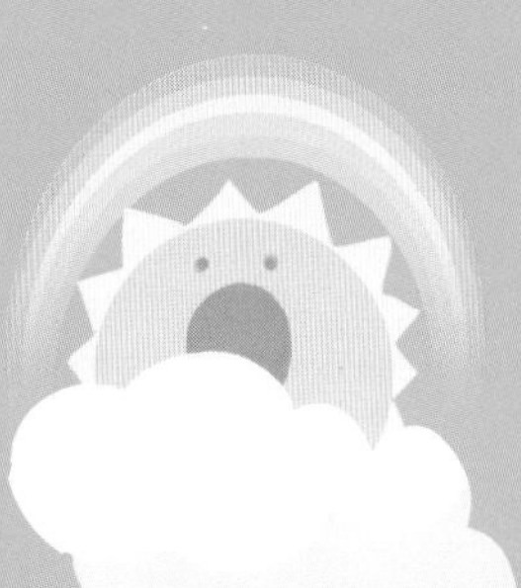

Look up on a clear day and you're sure to spot this kingdom from anywhere. Everyone knows the sun lives in the palace, but young magicians are more interested in Puffington's Academy for the Magically Gifted (and so on).

Folks from this kingdom have ears that curl up.

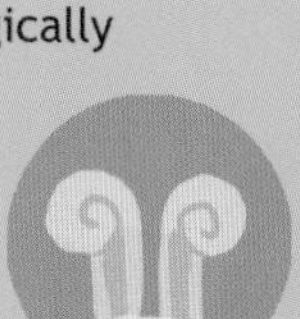

## The Space Kingdom

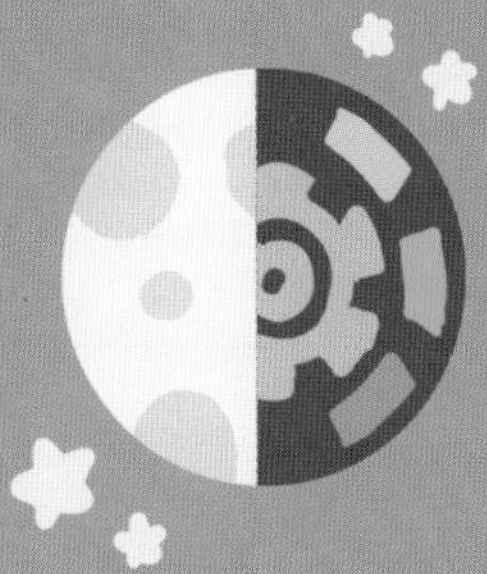

Also known as "the moon." A sophisticated computer keeps everything running smoothly in this futuristic society. Isn't it great how technology is so reliable?

Folks from this kingdom have wide ears with a symbol inside.

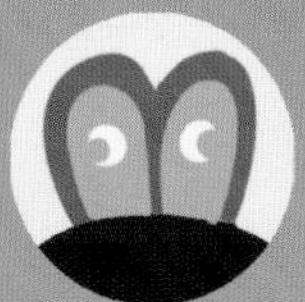

## ...and Beyond!

Dreamside's not the only planet in the galaxy, you know. The Space Kingdom frequently sees visitors from other worlds, and sometimes they have more than tourism on their minds.

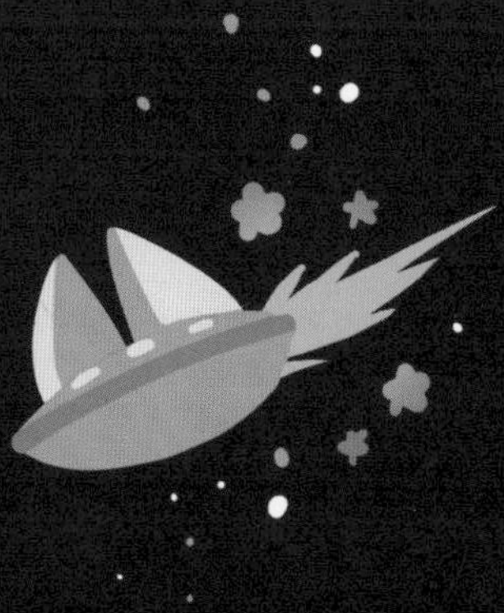

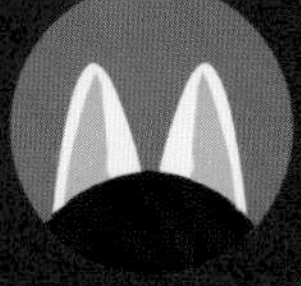

Generally, if someone doesn't have bunny ears, they may not be from Dreamside.

## ???

In some circles, there are whispers of another world parallel to Dreamside. No one knows how to get there or what might be waiting on the other side...

But do they really want to?

# Did you know...

...that somewhere in the busy streets of Caketown, there's an ice cream stand run by a girl named Neapolitan? With such fierce competition among other eateries, it's hard for her to attract much attention... but she's hoping to share her love for the best ice cream flavor(s) with all of Dreamside someday! Keep an eye out for her, okay?

# Of course you knew...

...that the first legendary hero sealed the Nightmare Knight away with the aid of the Dream Oracle many ages ago. But did you know his name was Gherkin? He also had a little sister named Peanut, who was basically there for moral support.

# You probably didn't need to know...

...that one of the most popular Doughnut Kingdom TV shows is *Food on Food*. In his search for the gnarliest eating challenge known to bunnyman, host Brisket Sweats has been banned from 278 different restaurants, much to the dismay of his cohost and nutritionist, Brussel Sprouts.

Yes, you didn't need to know this. But now you do.

# Concept Art

*Cucumber Quest* is a comic many years in the
making. Let's take a look at some steps along its
path from an early idea to the book you're holding!

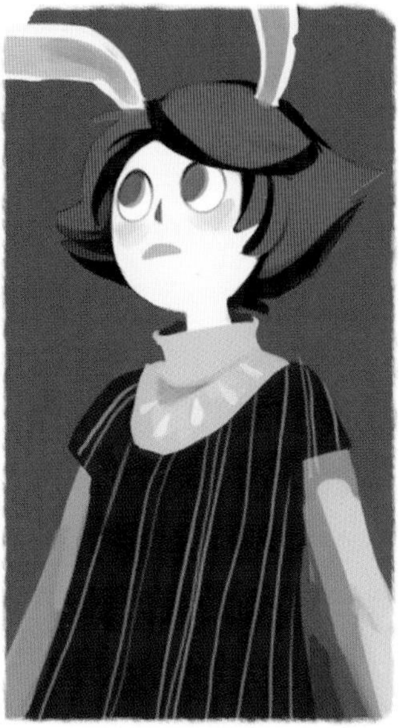
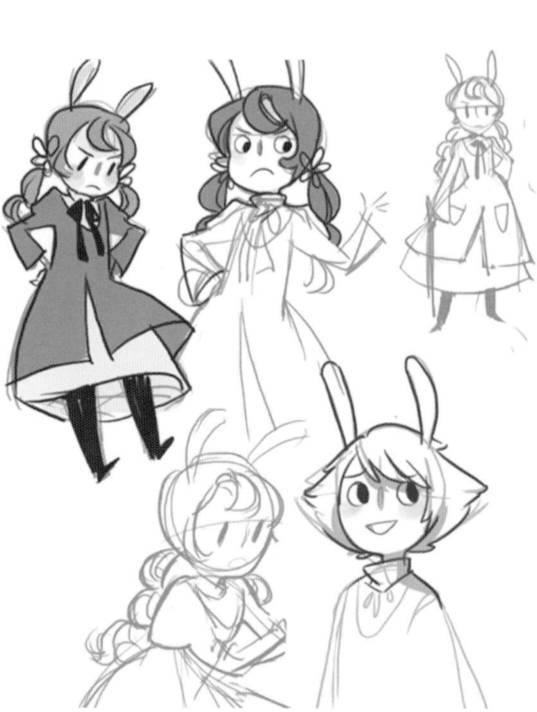
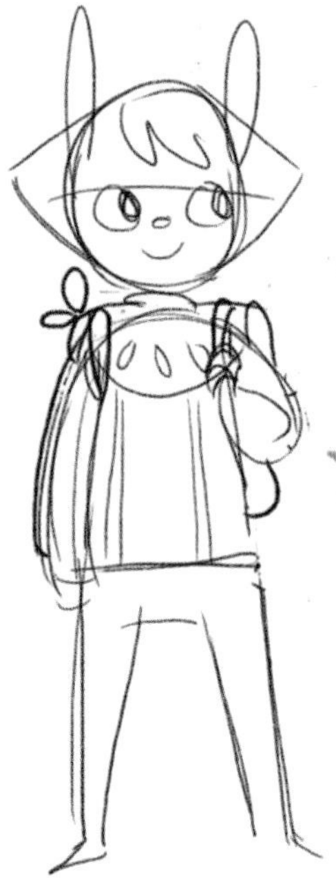
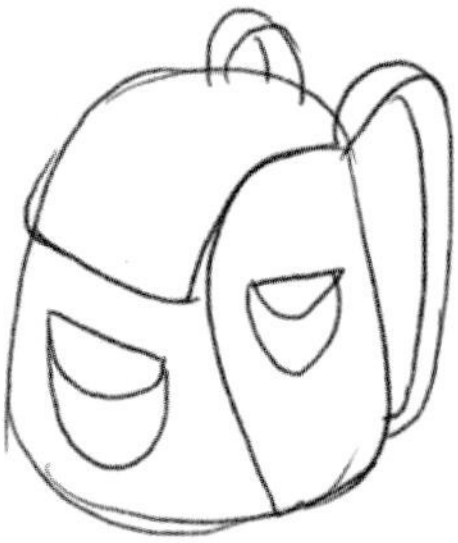
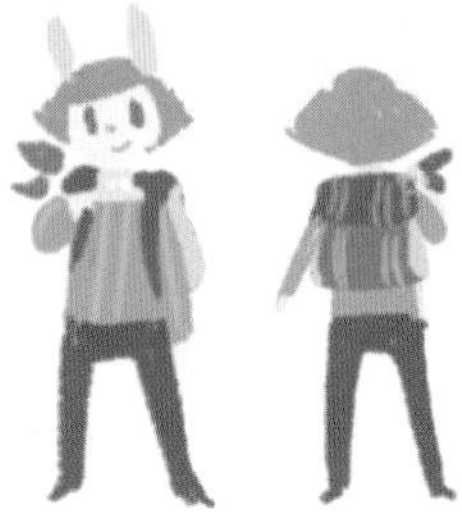
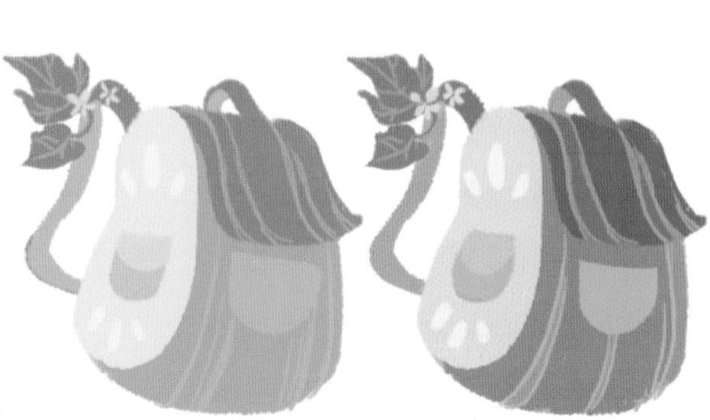

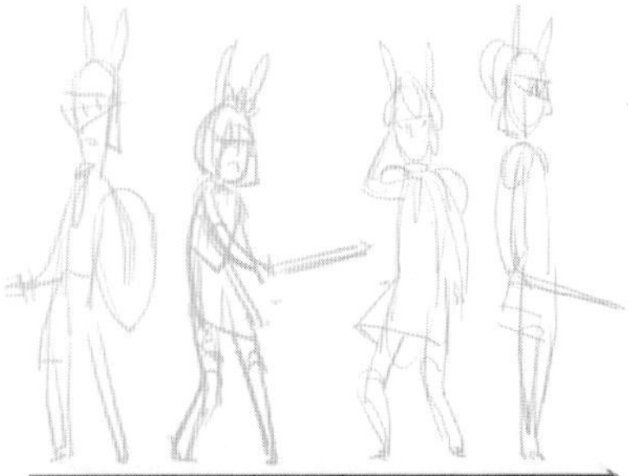

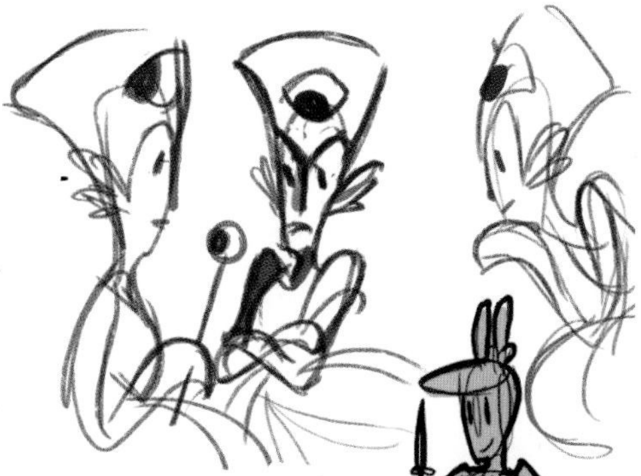

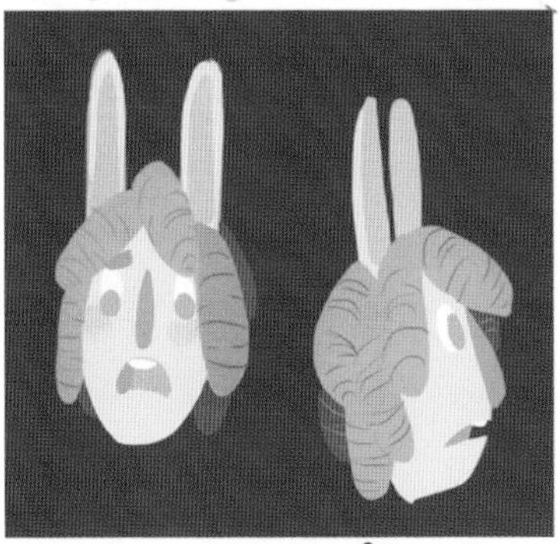

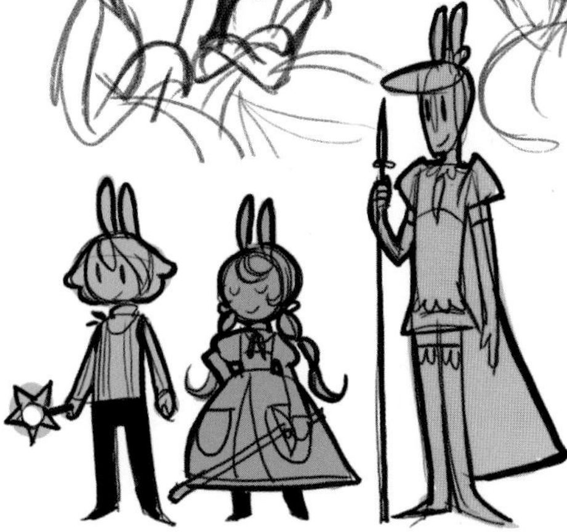

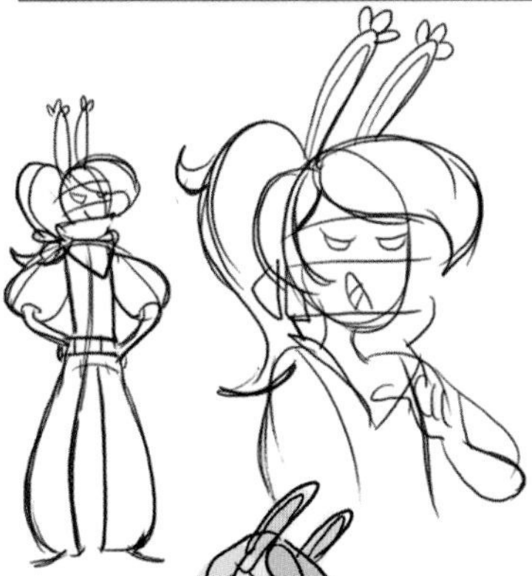

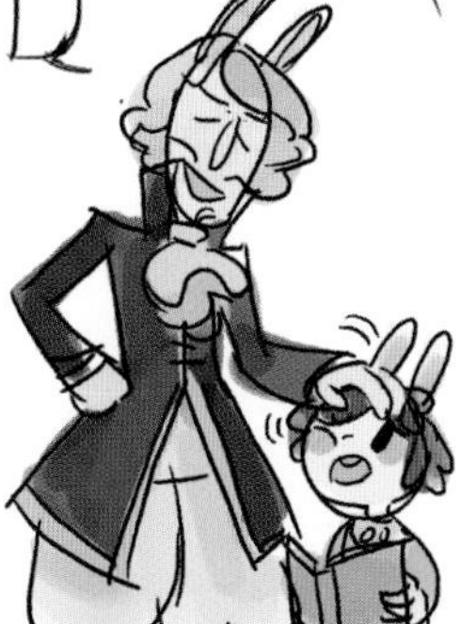

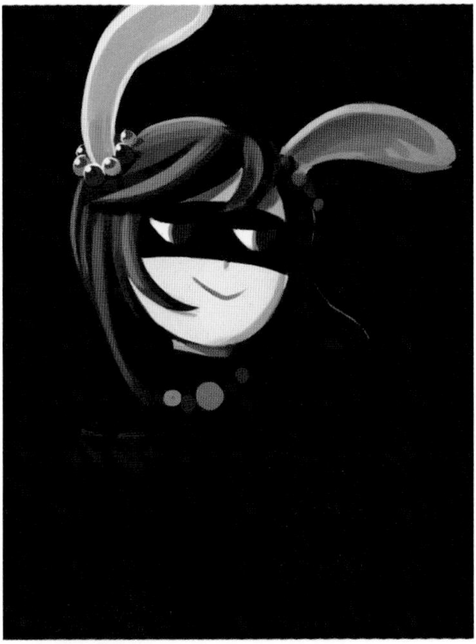

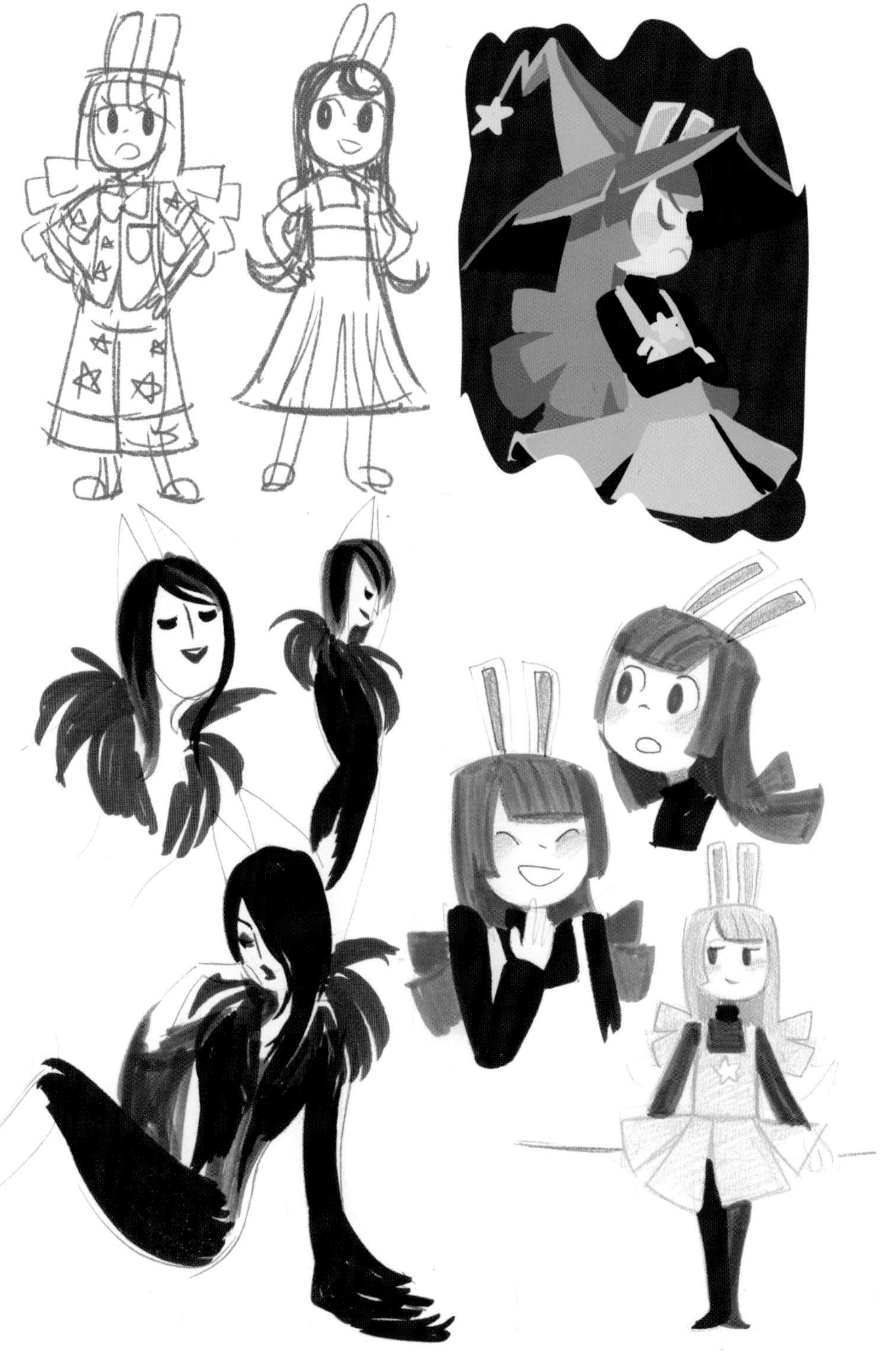

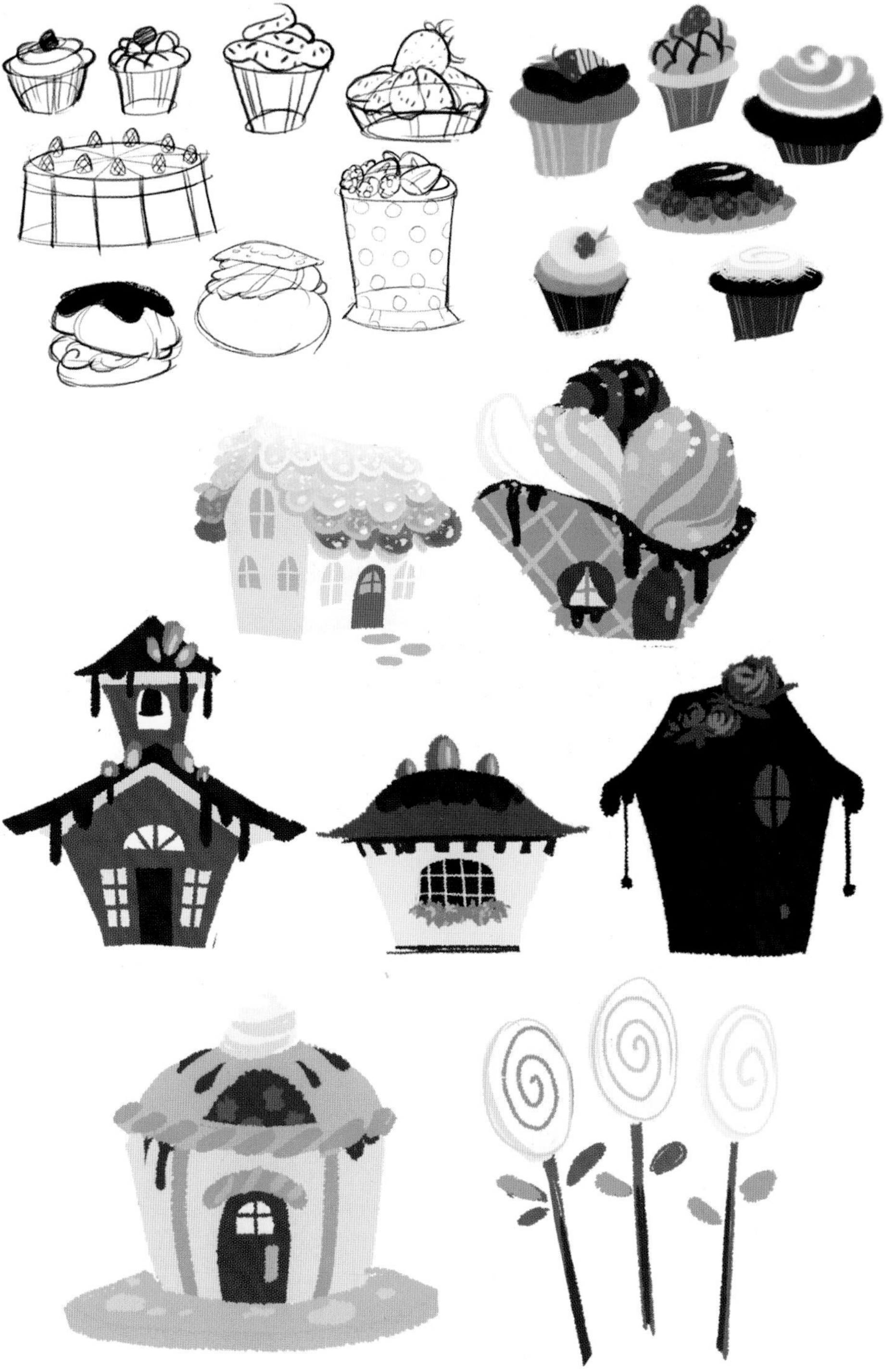

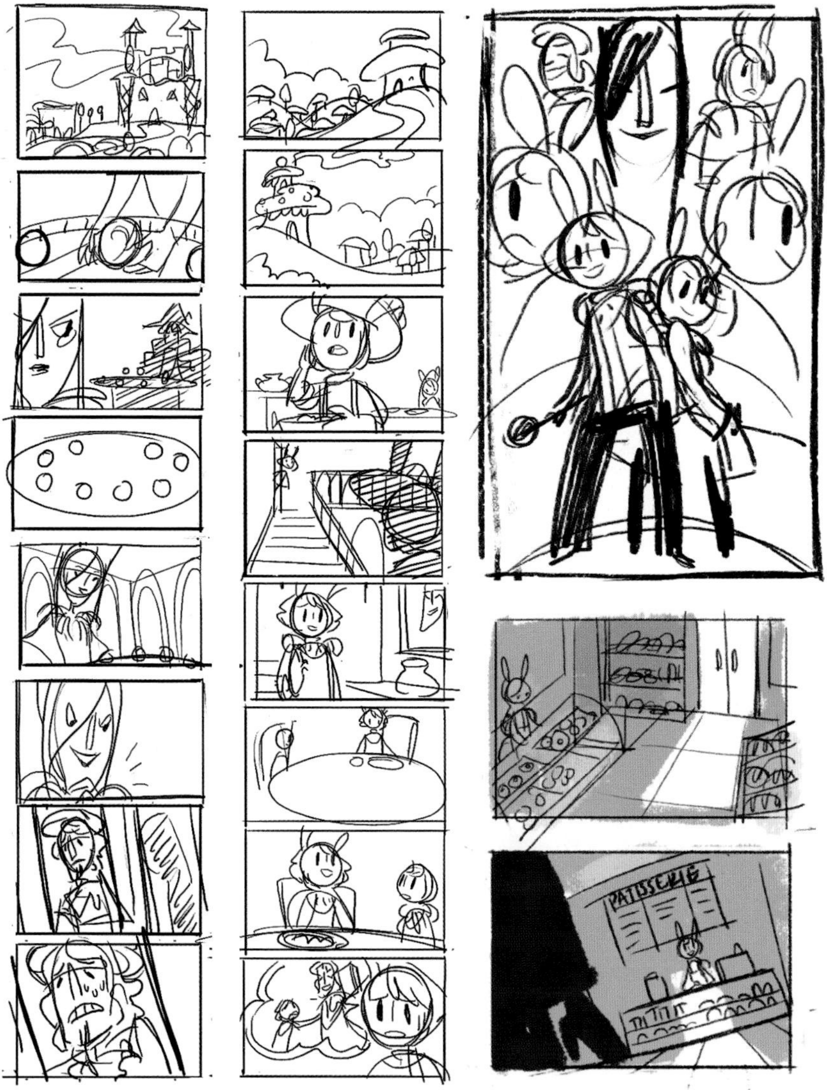
PATISSERIE

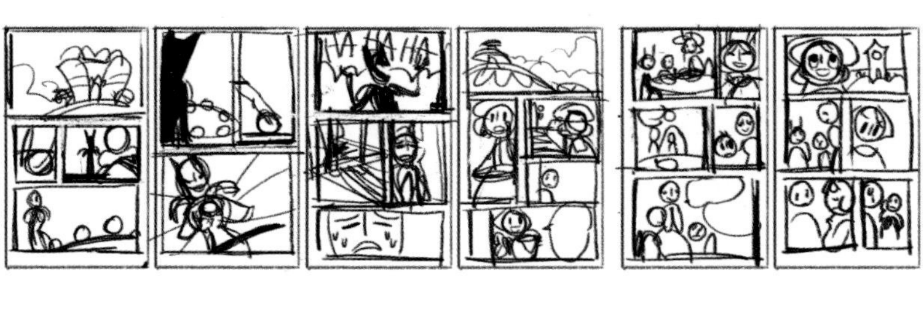

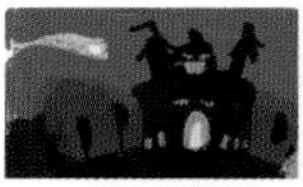
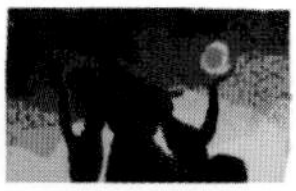
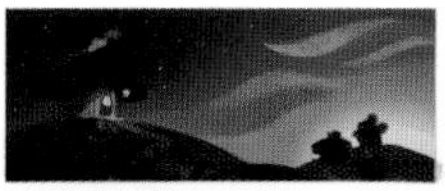
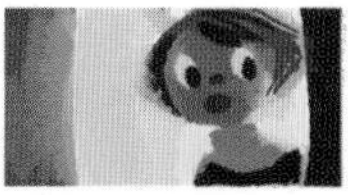
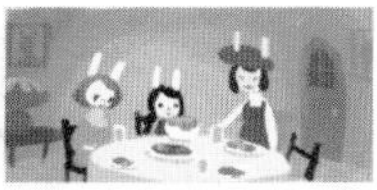
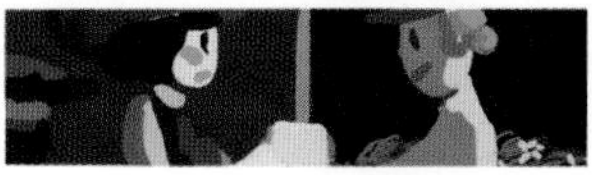
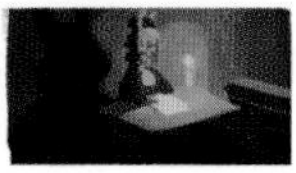
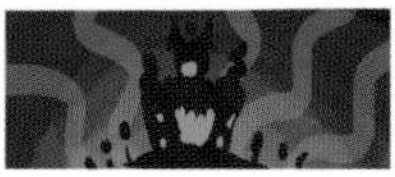
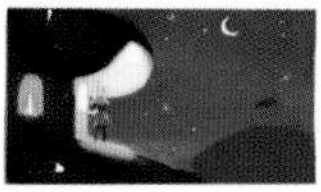
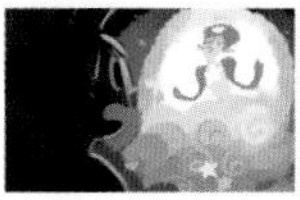
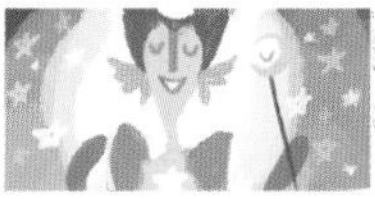
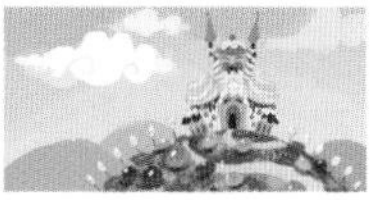
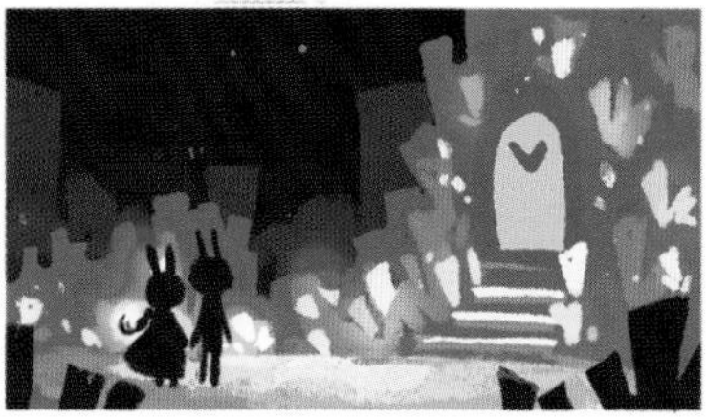
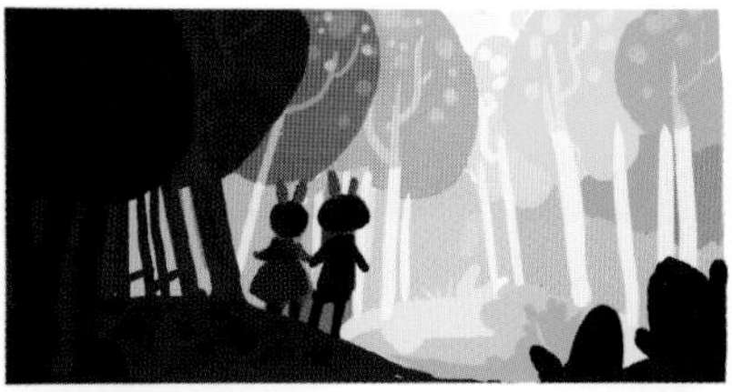
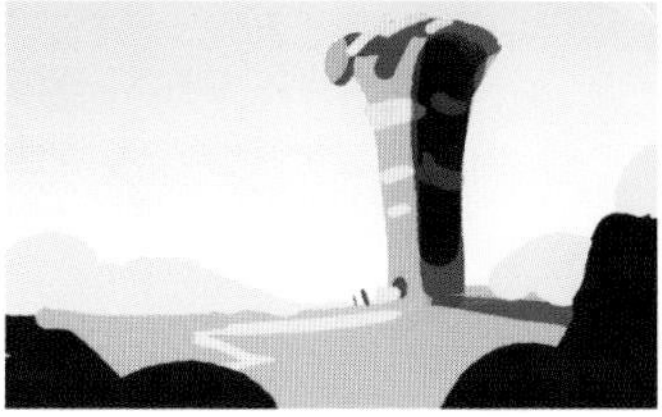
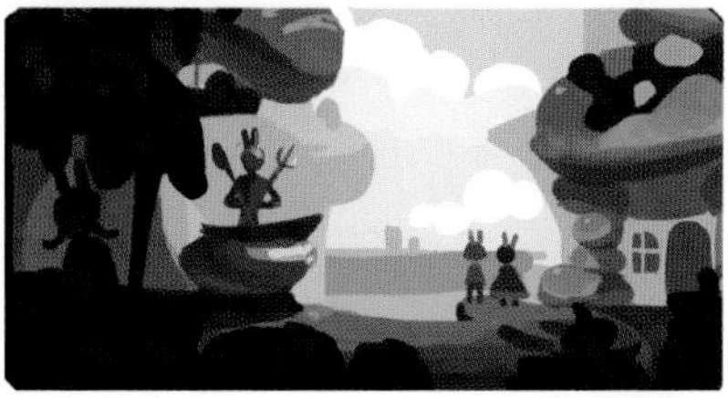
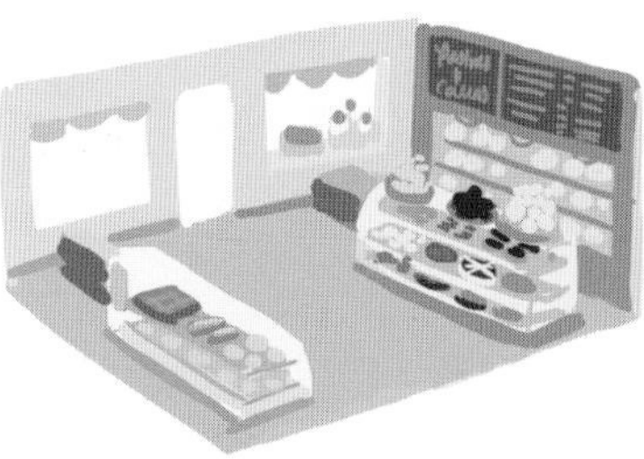
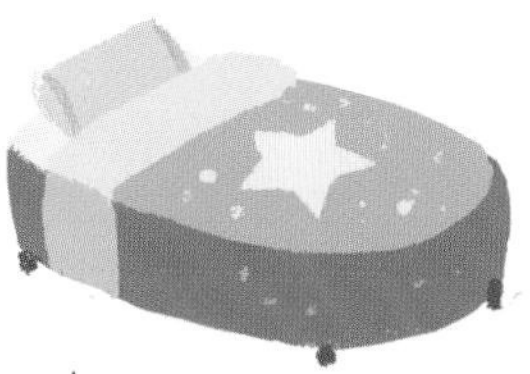
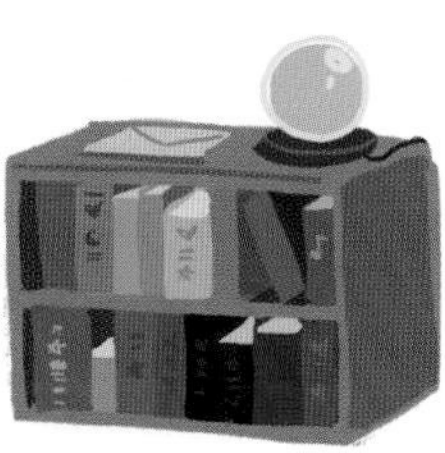
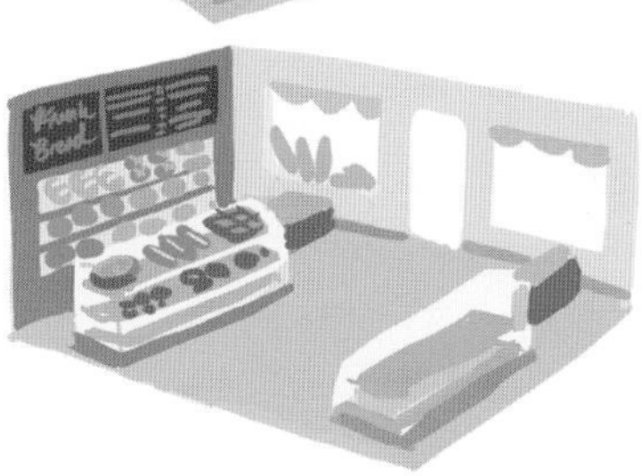
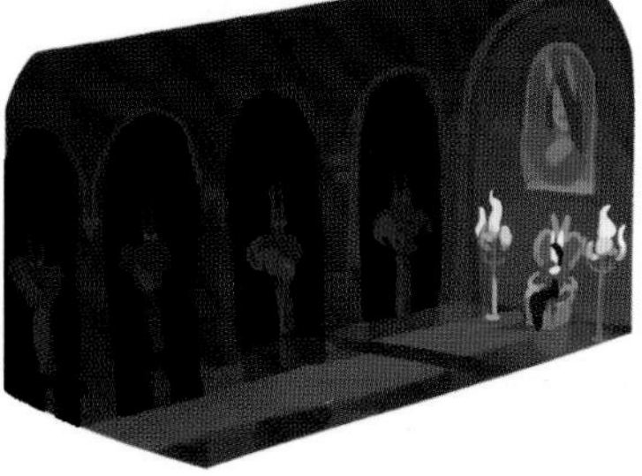

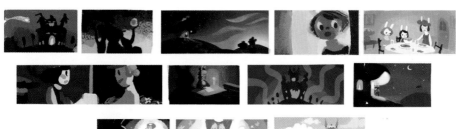

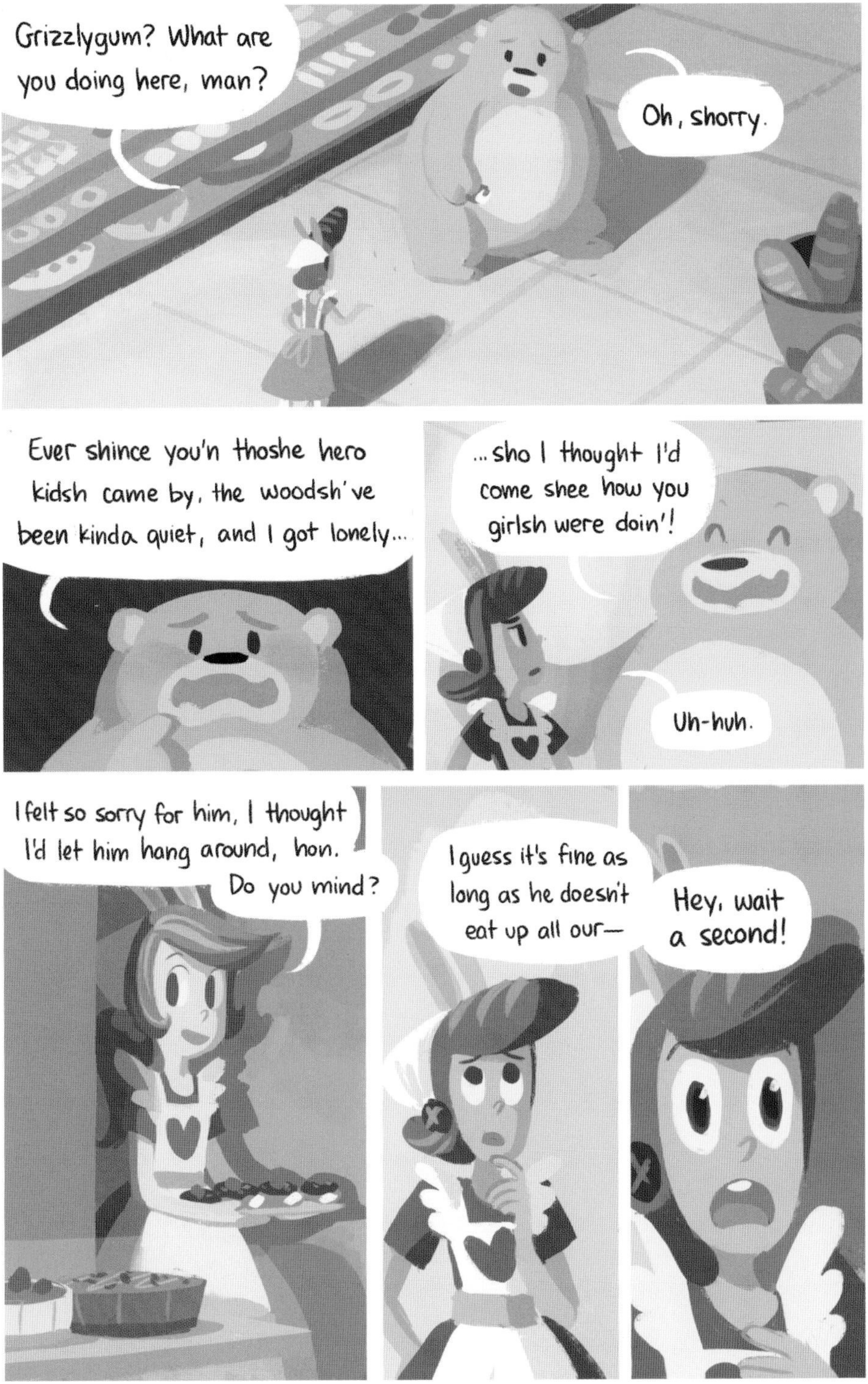
Grizzlygum? What are you doing here, man?
Oh, shorry.
Ever shince you'n thoshe hero kidsh came by, the woodsh've been kinda quiet, and I got lonely...
...sho I thought I'd come shee how you girlsh were doin'!
Uh-huh.
I felt so sorry for him, I thought I'd let him hang around, hon. Do you mind?
I guess it's fine as long as he doesn't eat up all our—
Hey, wait a second!

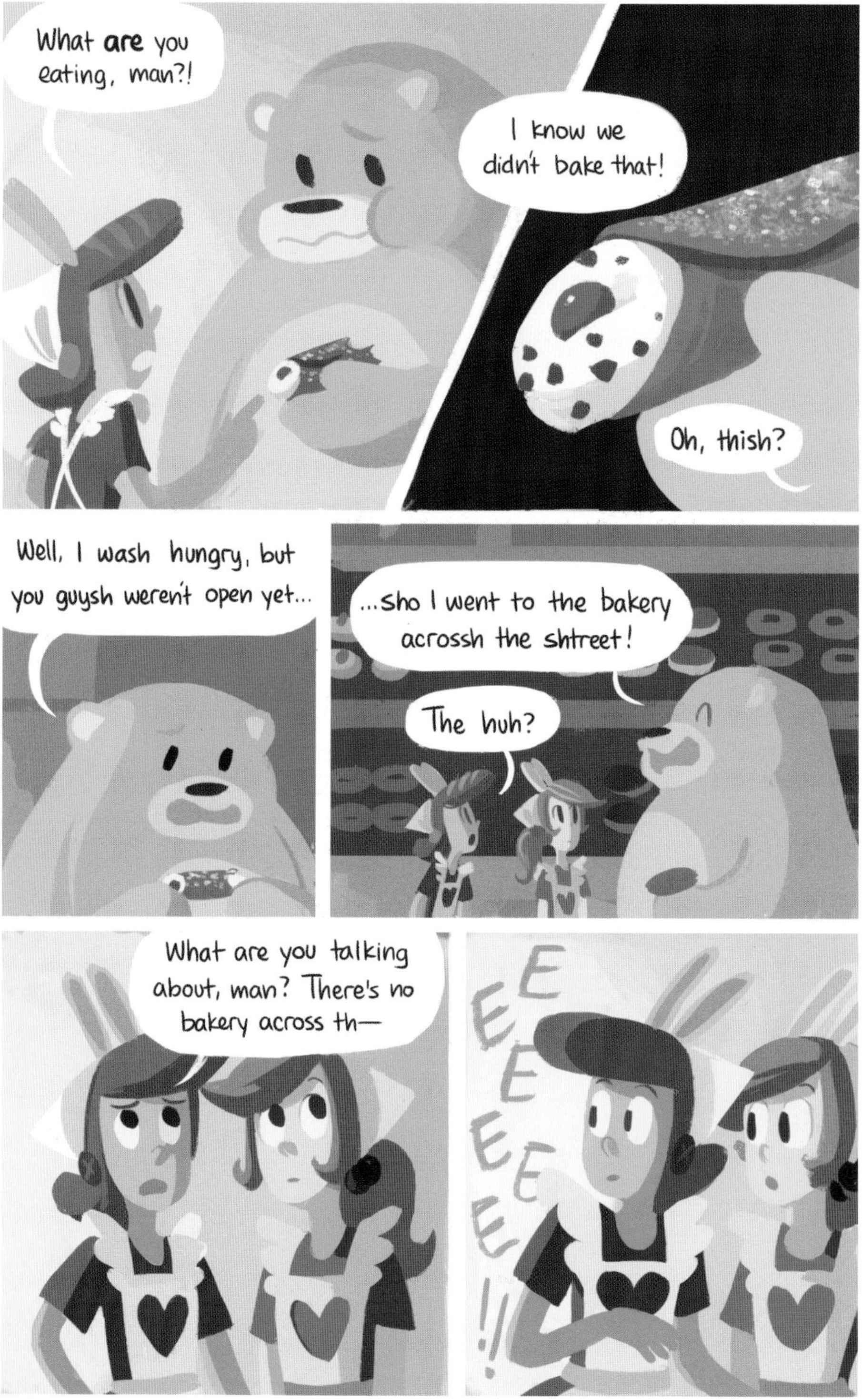
What **are** you eating, man?!
I know we didn't bake that!
Oh, thish?
Well, I wash hungry, but you guysh weren't open yet...
...sho I went to the bakery acrossh the shtreet!
The huh?
What are you talking about, man? There's no bakery across th—
EEEEEEEE!!

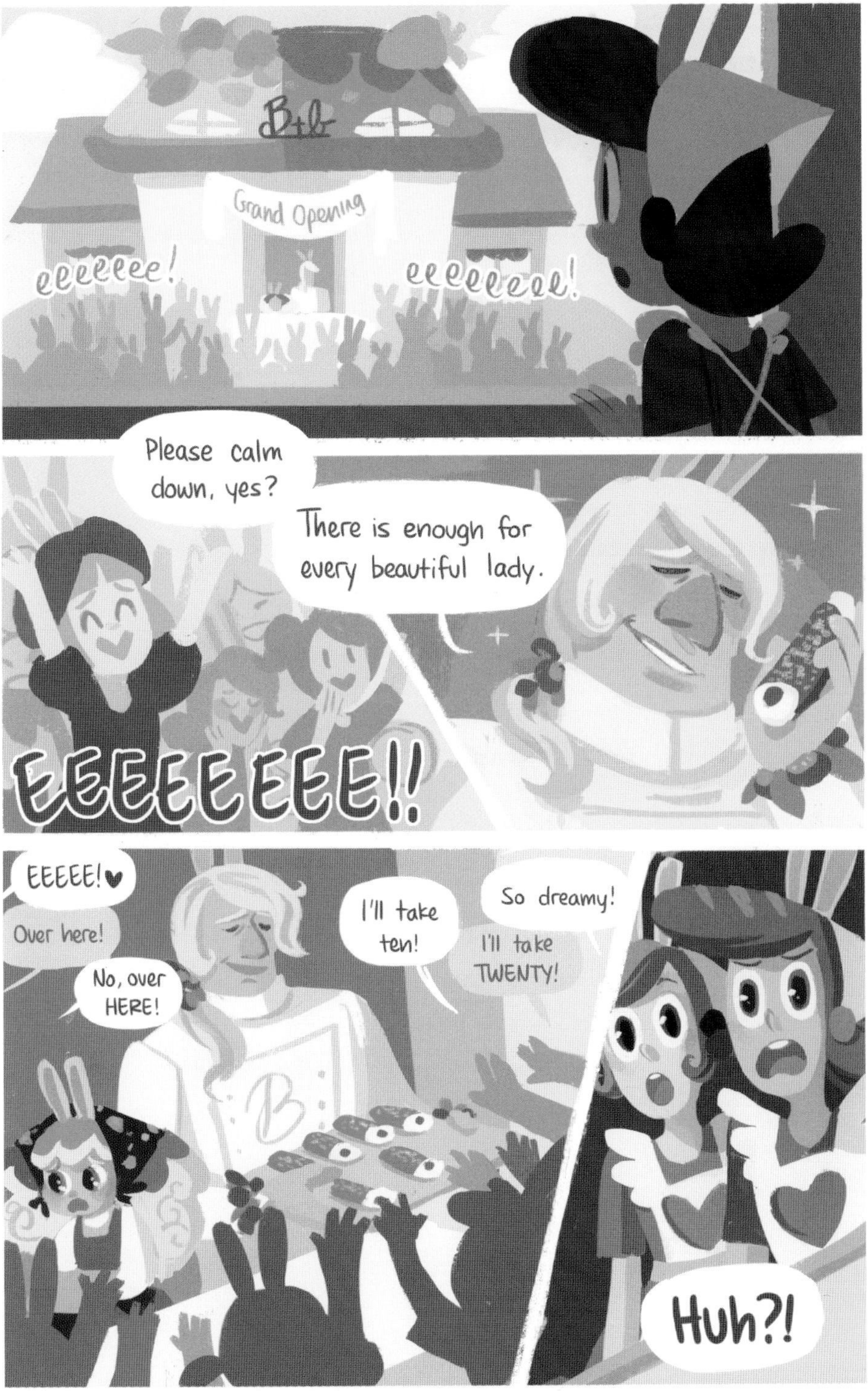
B+b
Grand Opening
eeeeee!
eeeeeeee!
Please calm down, yes?
There is enough for every beautiful lady.
EEEEEEEE!!
EEEEE!♥
Over here!
No, over HERE!
I'll take ten!
So dreamy!
I'll take TWENTY!
Huh?!

I am sorry. The competition, you see, she was not on Bruschetta's mind.

But, if our bakery is having more customers than yours...

What can we do, ah?

YOU WANNA TAKE THIS OUTSIDE OR WHAT

Baguette, no!

Big brother, these people are scary.

I know, Biscotti.

The sugar, we will get it somewhere else, yes?

Ciao!

shut.

I think you made an enemy, hon.

**HE** made an enemy when he set up shop!

There's no way I'm gonna let chumps like that run us out of business, man!

We've gotta fight back!

There's a reason the two of us won King's Best Bakery six years in a row,

and he's about to find out —

SM
MMPH
GRRMF
CHON

HOMF

186

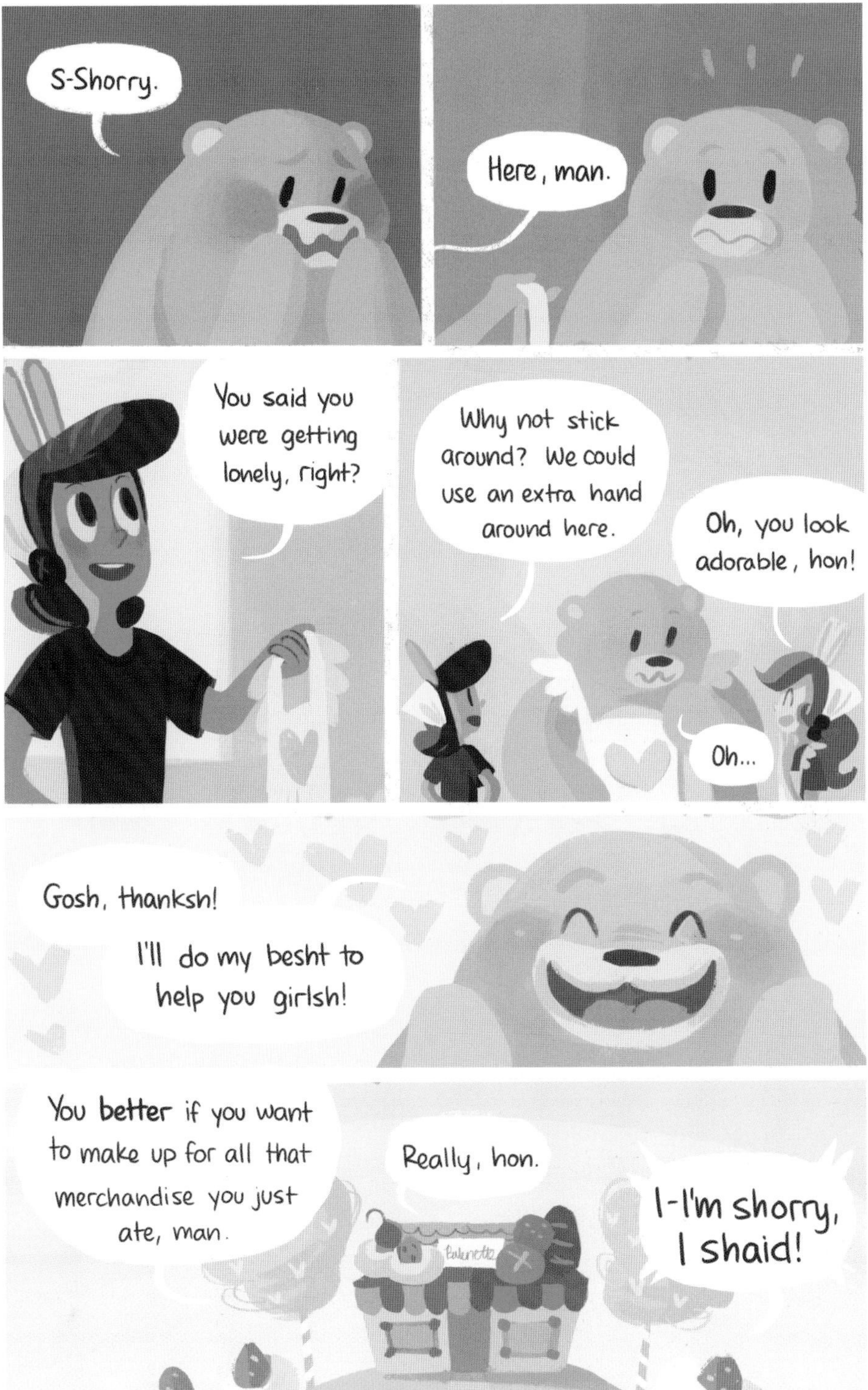
S-Shorry.
Here, man.
You said you were getting lonely, right?
Why not stick around? We could use an extra hand around here.
Oh, you look adorable, hon!
Oh...
Gosh, thanksh!
I'll do my besht to help you girlsh!
You better if you want to make up for all that merchandise you just ate, man.
Really, hon.
I-I'm shorry, I shaid!

# The Doughnut Kingdom

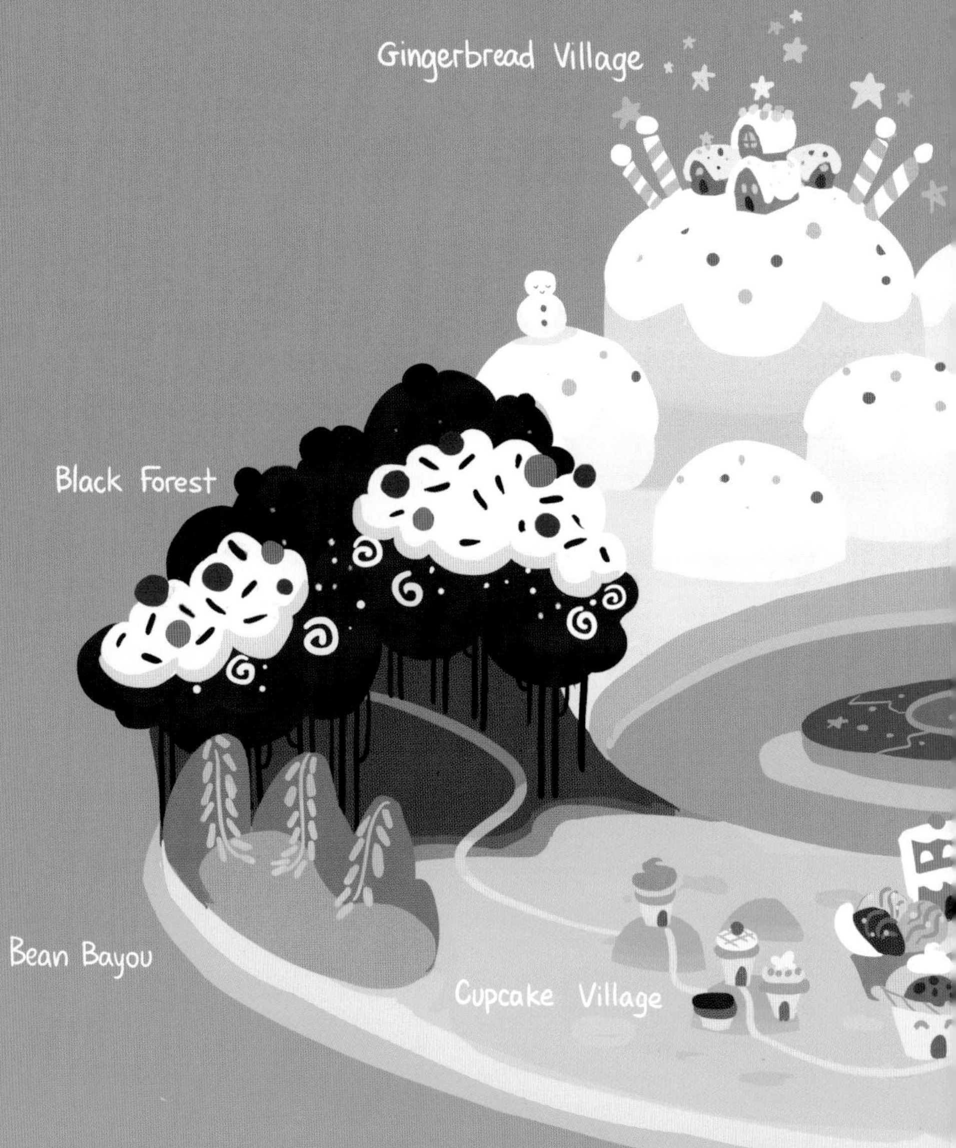
Gingerbread Village
Black Forest
Bean Bayou
Cupcake Village

Tiramisu Tower

Teacup Mountains

Saltine

Flatbread
Flatlands

Rock Candy Caves

Gumdrop Forest

Caketown

**First Second**

New York

Published by First Second
First Second is an imprint of Roaring Brook Press, a division of
Holtzbrinck Publishing Holdings Limited Partnership
175 Fifth Avenue, New York, New York 10010

Library of Congress Control Number: 2016961588

Paperback ISBN: 978-1-62672-832-5
Hardcover ISBN: 978-1-250-15803-1

Our books may be purchased in bulk for promotional, educational,
or business use. Please contact your local bookseller or the Macmillan
Corporate and Premium Sales Department at (800) 221-7945 ext. 5442
or by e-mail at MacmillanSpecialMarkets@macmillan.com.

First edition 2017
Book design by Rob Steen

Cucumber Quest is created entirely in Photoshop.

Printed in China by RR Donnelley Asia Printing Solutions Ltd.,
Dongguan City, Guangdong Province

Paperback: 10 9 8 7 6 5 4 3 2
Hardcover: 10 9 8 7 6 5 4 3 2